Uncle Sam's Boys in the Philippines

by H. Irving Hancock

CHAPTER I

THE FILIPINO DANDY

"We've solved one problem at last, Noll," declared Sergeant Hal Overton seriously.

"Only one?" demanded young Sergeant Terry quizzically.

But Hal, becoming only the more serious, went on earnestly:

"At last we begin to understand just what the 'lure of the Orient' means! For years I've been reading about the Orient, and the way that this part of the world charms men and holds them. Now, that we are here on the spot, I begin to understand it all. Noll, my boy, the East is a great and wonderful place! I wonder if I shall ever tire of it?"

"I believe I could tire of it in time," remarked Sergeant Terry, of the Thirty-fourth United States Infantry.

"But you haven't yet," insisted Sergeant Hal.

"What, when we've been here only three days? Naturally I haven't. And, besides, all we've seen is Manila, and certainly Manila can't be more than one little jumping-off corner of the Orient that you're so enthusiastic about."

"You're wild about the Far East, too—even the one little corner of it that we've seen," retorted Sergeant Hal. "Don't be a grouch or a knocker, Noll. Own up that you wouldn't start for the United States to-morrow if you were offered double pay back in the home country."

"No; I wouldn't," confessed Sergeant Terry. "I want to see a lot more of these Philippine Islands before I go back to our own land."

"Just halt where you are and look about you," went on enthusiastic Sergeant Hal. "Try to picture this scene as Broadway, in New York."

"Or Main Street in our own little home city," laughed Sergeant Terry quietly.

Certainly the scene was entirely different from anything that the two young Army boys had ever seen before.

They stood on the Escolta, which is the main business thoroughfare of New Manila, as that portion of the Philippine capital north of the little river is called. South of the river is Old Manila, the walled city of the old days of the Spanish conquerors. South of the walled city lie two rather fashionable residence suburbs, Ermita and Malate.

But the Thirty-fourth was temporarily stationed in big nipa barracks at Malate. It was in the newer Manila that the two boyish young sergeants found their greatest interest.

It was a busy, bustling scene. There is nothing exactly like the Escolta in any other part of the world. The whole of this crooked, winding thoroughfare seemed alive with horses and people—with the horses in more than goodly proportion.

Along the Escolta are the principal wholesale and retail houses of the city. Here is the post office, there the "Botanica" or principal drug store, operating under English capital and a Spanish name; down near the water front is the

Hotel de Paris, a place famous for the good dinners of the East. Further up the Escolta, just around a slight bend, is the Oriente Hotel, the stopping place of Army officers and their families, of passing travelers and of civil employees of the government.

At this point along the Escolta are the busiest marts of local trade. The sidewalks are crowded with hurrying throngs; the streets jammed with traffic, for in Manila few of the whites or the wealthier natives ever think of walking more than a block or two. The *quilez*, the little two-wheeled car drawn by a six-hundred-pound pony, is the common means of getting about. A dollar in American money will charter one of these *quilez* for hours, and the heat renders it an advisable investment for one who has far to go.

Automobiles were scarce, though they had penetrated even this congested Escolta. Here and there an Army officer or orderly appeared on horseback in the crush of the street. If he attempted to ride at a canter the horseman seemed to be taking his life in his own hands, with the chances all against him.

Save for the lazy calls of drivers—*cocheros*—to their horses, the hum of human voices was subdued. In the heat of the Escolta the people of all colors seem to have reached a tacit understanding that it requires less exertion to talk in low tones.

White people of both sexes appeared, clad usually in the white attire so customary in the tropics. Filipino dandies affected the same garbing, with the exception of here and there a natty, nervous, little brown man who appeared in the more formal black frock coat. But few, even of these, had the courage to come out in sun-up hours wearing the silk hat that is the usual accompaniment of the long-tailed frock coat.

Despite the heat, the faces of most of the people in the crowded streets appeared cheerful, even happy. Life is not taken too seriously in the Orient. The natives always find plenty of time for laughter; the stranger soon acquires the trick.

Banks, stores, restaurants, mineral water kiosks—all the places of resort along the Escolta—were abundantly patronized, yet none save the *cocheros* perched up on the little seats of the *quilez* appeared to be at all in a hurry.

Yet one man in particular appeared to be devoid of hurry. In fact, he paused or halted whenever the two boyish young sergeants did. He invariably kept about a hundred feet behind them in this queerly bustling yet ever leisurely crowd that thronged the sidewalks of the Escolta.

While Hal and Noll were curiously noting the fact—that the Escolta seems always so busy, but the individuals who make up the life there seem never in a hurry—the man who was plainly following them never glanced at them directly, yet never once lost sight of them.

Neither Hal nor Noll had yet noted the man, about whom there were some points that would have been amusing to the American youngsters.

This man was a Filipino. At first glance one would have believed him to be a Tagalo, or member of the most warlike and ambitious of all the eighty-odd tribes that make up the peoples of these islands. The Tagalos are the tribe most frequently found in and around Manila, and in the provinces nearest to that city.

In appearance the Tagalos look a good deal like underfed Japanese. It was to the Tagalos that the *insurrecto* leader, Aguinaldo, belonged.

These Tagalos, however, consider themselves in every way the equals and match for any white man. The Tagalos have absorbed much of the Spanish civilization. Many of them are wealthy and the sons of such families generally hold degrees from Philippine colleges. Well-to-do Tagalos, despite their undersized stature and dark-brown skins, affect all the culture—and the vices—of well-to-do white people. They conduct banks, engage in commerce, mingle with white society, and consider themselves as bright lights of civilization. Above all, every Tagalo takes keen interest in politics. Yet these Tagalos, up to date, are only veneered Malays.

This Filipino who was so patiently following Sergeants Hal and Noll appeared to belong to the well-to-do class. Certainly he was an immaculate dandy. He was about five feet two inches in height, and wore neat-fitting, well-tailored white duck garments. The blouse was buttoned down in front, a military, braided white collar standing up stiffly, rendering the wearing of a shirt unnecessary. On his feet were highly polished tan shoes of American make. On his head he wore a jaunty, straight-brimmed straw hat of the best native manufacture. In his right hand this irreproachable Filipino dandy lightly swung a feather-weight bamboo cane.

His eyes were dark, gleaming, intense—fitted either to reflect laughter or sharp anger. But what rendered this man, who appeared to be close to thirty-five years of age, ridiculous to American eyes was his mustache. This was blue-black in color, waxed to two fine, bristling, upturned points—a fashion that this dandy had undoubtedly caught from some former Spanish military officer.

"They are boys—they will suit my purpose excellently," murmured the Filipino to himself, as he halted before a window where tropical outfittings for men were attractively displayed. Yet, though he gazed in at the window, he saw Sergeants Hal and Noll out of the corners of his eyes. "They are young, ambitious; they are enlisted men, therefore poor. Even in this short time these boys must have learned the craving for the things that money alone will buy. No man, in the Orient, can escape that knowledge and that longing for money. That is why it is so easy to buy men's souls here in the East. Shall I go up and speak to them? But no! There they go into a curio store where they will find much that they may wish to buy. I will follow my young *sergentes* inside in five minutes— or ten. *Then* they will be ripe for the man who talks money."

Hal and Noll had entered one of the most attractive little shops to be found anywhere along the Escolta. This store is kept by a Chinaman, who sells the more costly curios of the Far East. China's choicest silks are here displayed; also her finest teakwoods and curious boxes and cabinets of sandal and other valued woods, inlaid with pearl, or studded with rare jades. Here are wonderful creations carved out of ivory, idols of all kinds and sizes, of the highest grades of artistic workmanship. Here are wonderful beaded portieres and the most costly of curious Chinese garments for women. In a word, the bazaars of China are nobly represented on the Escolta. But there is much more besides. The most attractive curios from India, from Ceylon, the Malay Peninsula and of native

Filipino workmanship are all to be found here. It is not the place to enter when one has not much money.

No wonder Sergeant Overton and Sergeant Terry moved from counter to counter, pricing and sighing. Each young Army boy wanted to send home something worth while to his mother. Yet how small a sergeant's pay seems in such a bazaar!

Hal Overton and Noll Terry need no introduction to the reader of the earlier volumes in this series. "Uncle Sam's Boys in the Ranks," as our readers are aware, details how Hal and Noll, reared in love of the Flag and respect for the military, determined, at the age of eighteen, to enlist in the Regular Army. Our readers followed the new recruits to the recruit rendezvous, where the young men received their first drillings in the art of being a soldier. From there they followed Hal and Noll westward, to Fort Clowdry, in the Colorado mountains, where the young soldiers went through their first thrilling experiences of the strenuous side of Army life, proving themselves, whether in barracks, on drill ground or under fire on a lonely sentry post, to be the sort of American youths of whom the best soldiers are made.

Readers of "Uncle Sam's Boys on Field Duty" already know how Hal and Noll went several steps further in learning the work of the soldier; of their surprisingly good and highly adventurous work in practical problems of field life. In this volume was described field life and outpost duty, and scouting duty as well, as they are actually taught in the Army. In this volume is told also how Hal and Noll while out with a scouting party supplied their company with unexpected bear meat. Our readers, too, will remember the thrilling work of Hal and Noll, under Lieutenant Prescott, in capturing a desperate character badly wanted by the state authorities. These young soldiers were heroes of other absorbing adventures; their fine work eventually leading to their appointments as corporals.

In "Uncle Sam's Boys As Sergeants" our readers will recall a host of happenings that belong to military life, among them the stirring military tournament in which a battalion of "Ours" took part at Denver, and the all but tragic results of that tournament; the soldier hunting-party up in the Rockies, in which Hal and Noll thoroughly distinguished themselves both as hunters and as soldiers and commanders.

And now we find the entire Thirty-fourth Infantry in Manila, stationed there briefly pending details at other points in the islands.

As we look in upon Sergeants Overton and Terry to-day we find them two years older than when they first enlisted—but many years older in all the fine qualities that go to make up the best manhood.

Either young sergeant's word was as good as his bond in the Thirty-fourth. Truthful, ambitious, manly, thoroughly trained and capable of commanding; in a word, *men* in character and abilities, while yet boys in years.

This much had two years of life in the United States Army done for Hal Overton and Noll Terry. Could other training have done more?

And these were the young Americans whom the alert-eyed, trailing Filipino dandy had already singled out and had planned to corrupt to his own purposes.

Yet the astute man of the world knows more than one way of ruining and disgracing simple-hearted, true-souled young fellows. Not even Satan is credited with appearing often in evil guise at first.

Perhaps this Filipino, a wicked fellow of long training, knew how to go about his work.

"Going to buy anything, Noll?" asked Hal at last, after the two young sergeants had made the round of the bewildering, attractive store.

"I would, if I could find anything worth while that didn't take a sergeant's whole year's pay," sighed Terry.

"Things are fearfully dear here, aren't they?" murmured Overton. "Yet I want to send something home as a remembrance to mother."

"What do you fancy most?" asked Noll.

"If you haven't anything else on your mind, come around and I'll show you," Hal proposed.

Nodding, Noll accompanied his chum. Hal stopped to rest one hand lightly on a very wonderful little chest, made out of teak and sandal woods. It was richly, wonderfully carved, the darker teakwood being also inlaid with pearl. Inside were compartments and drawers, including two little secret drawers that the smiling Chinese salesman artfully opened and exposed to view.

"One all same fo' *dinero* (money), other fo' plecious stones, jewels, you *sabe*," cooed the yellow attendant.

"It's a beauty and a wonder," murmured Hal. "Mother'd be the proudest woman in town if I could send it home to her. How much did you say it cost?"

"Him tloo hundled pesos," stated the Chinaman gravely.

A *peso* is the Spanish name for a Mexican dollar, worth about forty-seven cents; but two *pesos* and an American dollar are reckoned as of the same value in Manila.

"A hundred dollars gold! Why, that's the same price you asked me before," cried Hal in good-natured protest.

"Yep, allee same; him plenty cheap."

"It's too much," sighed Sergeant Hal. But the Chinaman, as though he had not heard, asked:

"You likee? You buy?"

"I can't afford it at that price."

"All light; come in some other day," invited the Chinaman politely, and glided over to where another possible customer was examining some handsome jade jewelry.

"My *soldado* (soldier) friend has not been long in Manila?" inquired a low, pleasant, courteous voice behind the two young soldiers.

Hal wheeled. It was the Filipino dandy whom he confronted. That smiling, prosperous-looking native was employing his left hand to twist one end of the upturned moustache to a finer point.

"No; we haven't been here long," Hal smiled. "Three days, in fact."

"And you do not yet know how to bargain with these sharp-witted *Chinos* (Chinese)?"

"I'm afraid not," said Sergeant Overton.

"May I ask, señor, what you wished to buy?"

"This box," Hal answered.

"And how much did the *Chino* want for it, if I may make bold enough to ask so much of the señor's business?"

"Why, he wants a hundred dollars in gold," Hal responded.

The Filipino dandy inspected the box critically.

"You are right, señor; the price is too high. It is *muy caro* (very dear), in fact. It could be bought for less, if you knew better how to deal with these smiling yellow heathen."

"I'd be greatly obliged, then, if you would tell me how to put the bargain through."

"You should get this rare and handsome box, señor, for ninety dollars, gold— even, perhaps, for not much more than eighty."

"Even that would be a fearful price for me to pay," murmured Hal, shaking his head regretfully. "I shall have to give up the idea, I guess."

"Ah, but no!" cried the Filipino, as though struck suddenly by an idea. "Not if the señor will do me one very great favor!"

"What favor can I possibly do you?" asked Sergeant Hal, regarding the little brown man with considerable astonishment.

"Why, it is all very simple, señor. Simply let me feel that I have been permitted to do a courtesy to an *Americano* to one of the race to which I owe so much. In a word, señor, I am not—as you may perhaps guess"—here the Filipino swelled slightly with a pride that was plain—"I am not exactly a poor man, not since the *Americanos* came to these islands and gave us the blessings of liberty and just government. I have many business ventures, and one of them lies in my being a secret—no, what you *Americanos* call a silent partner of the *Chino* who conducts this store. Now the favor that I ask—señor, I beg you to let me present you with this handsome little box, that you may send it over the waters to your sweetheart."

"Make me a present of it?" demanded Sergeant Hal in amazement.

"Ah, yes, exactly so, señor; and I shall be greatly honored by your very kind acceptance. And your friend—he shall select anything—valuable and handsome—that he would like for his sweetheart."

Neither young sergeant had a sweetheart outside of his mother. It was for their mothers that they sought suitable-priced curios. In their amazement, however, neither Hal nor Noll took the trouble to correct this smiling, polite stranger.

"Thank you," said Overton promptly. "We can't accept, of course, though it is very kind of you to make the offer—so very kind that it almost takes our breath away."

"And why can you not accept?" insisted the Filipino. He was still smiling, but there was now something so insistent in his voice that Noll answered quickly:

"Because we cannot accept gifts from strangers."

"Ah, but you do not yet know the Orient. You must have things here; you must have money to spend, and feel the pleasure of spending it, or you will die."

"Thank you," laughed Sergeant Hal, "but at present my health is excellent. As for dying, that has no terror for the soldier."

8

"Ah, yes, to die like a soldier!" protested the Filipino, with a shrug of his shoulders. "But would you die of sheer weariness and envy? There are pleasures in this country which only money will buy. Without the money, without these pleasures, life soon becomes bitter. You do not know, but I do, for I have watched thousands of your *Americano* soldiers here. Now, I have money—too much! It is my whim to see that the *soldados* enjoy themselves. I have begged many a soldier to honor me by letting me purchase him a little pleasure. Come, I will show you now! Wait! I will send for a carriage—not a *quilez,* but a victoria. Say the word, give the consent, and I will show you at once what is called pleasure here in the East—in Manila."

Though he spoke in low tones, the Filipino made almost extravagant gestures. As he kept on he warmed up to his subject.

"Shall I call a victoria?" he asked.

"If you wish," replied Sergeant Hal dryly.

"Ah, that is the way I like to hear you say it!" cried the little Filipino, and hastened toward the door.

He went away so rapidly, in fact, that he did not have time to note young Sergeant Overton's altered manner. From a feeling of embarrassment over having to repulse a stranger's ill-advised offer of generosity, Hal, his eyes watching the man's face, speedily took a dislike to the Filipino.

"Come along, Noll," Overton whispered. "We'll get out of this. I don't like the fellow."

"You like him as well as I do," muttered Sergeant Terry.

At the door of the store they again caught sight of the dandy, who, with hand extended, was at that moment signaling a *cochero* to drive his victoria in to the curb.

"It could not have been better," cried the little brown tempter. "Just as I came out I saw an empty victoria."

"I congratulate you," smiled Sergeant Hal.

"No, but this is the carriage, here," cried the Filipino, as Hal and Noll turned to walk down the Escolta.

"Get in, then, and enjoy yourself," called back Hal.

In an instant the Filipino was in front of them, barring their way.

"But you permitted me to stop a carriage," he protested, bewildered.

"Exactly," nodded Hal, "and we hope you will enjoy yourself. Step aside, please, for we want to pass on."

"But you are not going with me, after——"

"Nothing was said about that," Hal answered, "and we have other plans. Good-bye."

As the Filipino dandy once more tried to place himself in front of the young sergeant, Hal gently but firmly thrust the insistent fellow aside.

The Filipino stood glaring after them until the two Army boys were out of sight. The glint in his eyes was far from pleasant.

"Now, what on earth did that fellow want of us?" demanded Noll wonderingly.

"Nothing good, anyway," returned Hal Overton. "Intending benefactors don't act in that fashion. He may represent a bad phase of life out here. Let's forget him. Say, here's a store we must have overlooked on our way up here. Let's go in."

Half an hour later the Army boys came out of the store, each carrying a small parcel. For his first present home each young soldier had bought for his mother a small assortment of the wonderfully filmy *pina* lace handkerchiefs made by the native women.

"No *quilez* around here for hire," said Hal, after looking up and down the Escolta. "Let's walk across the bridge over the Pasig. We'll be more likely to find an idle *cochero* on the other side of the river."

As they started the sky was darkening, and the lightning beginning to flash, for this was in early July, at the height of the rainy season.

"I hope we find a *cochero* soon," muttered Noll, looking up at the dark sky. "I don't fancy the idea of walking all the way out to Malate in a downpour."

They were not quite over the bridge when the storm broke in all its force. Tropical thunder crashed with a fury that made artillery fire seem trifling. Great sheets of lightning flashed on all sides.

"Hustle, before we get drowned," laughed Sergeant Hal, breaking into a fast run. "There's shelter just beyond the end of the bridge."

The shelter for which both soldiers headed was a kiosk, barely larger than a sentry-box, that had once been erected for the convenience of the native boys who stood there with relief horses for the service of the old street car line.

The door stood open. Eager to make any port in a storm, Hal and Noll bolted inside just in time to hear an angry voice declare:

"I had them picked out—two young *sergentes*, mere boys. At first they were very polite—a minute later they made fun of me to my face—me, Vicente Tomba! But I shall know them again, I shall see them, and I shall make them wish they had never been born. I——"

The Filipino dandy stopped short as the two Army boys stepped briskly inside. He gave a gasp as he recognized them.

"We meet again," remarked Hal dryly.

The dandy's companion, a big, florid-faced man of forty, in the usual immaculate white duck of the white man, eyed the boys keenly.

CHAPTER II

A MEETING AT THE NIPA BARRACKS

It was only for a moment.

Then, without answering Hal's remark, the Filipino clutched at the white man's arm, shoving him out into the rain. The native followed.

Just then a *cochero* with an empty *quilez* drove up. With instant presence of mind Vicente Tomba, as the dandy had called himself, held up his hand.

It was all done in an instant, and native and white friend were driving away through the gusts of rain.

"Wonder who our friends are?" Noll remarked curiously.

"We know that one of them calls himself Vicente Tomba," replied Sergeant Hal.

"But he spoke of having us picked out for something, and he seemed almost peevish because we didn't suit him," smiled Noll.

"I can't imagine what it is," replied Hal, undisturbed. "It couldn't be anything in the high treason line, anyway."

"Why not even that?" demanded Sergeant Noll.

"Why, look here, old fellow, we're just two plain, kid, doughboy sergeants of the line. If that fellow had wanted anything in the treasonable variety, what sort of goods could we deliver him, anyway? Nothing, much, beyond our own arms and a copy of the company's roll."

"Then what on earth was the fellow up to, anyway?"

"I don't know, Noll, and I don't much care. I've heard that there are sharks of all sorts here in Manila, ready to put up all sorts of games to get the easy-mark soldier's pay away from him. Probably Tomba and his friend belong in that class."

"Pooh! Tomba has plenty of money," snorted Noll Terry. "He wouldn't have to be out for a poor, buck-foot soldier's pay."

"Swindlers sometimes do have plenty of money, for a while, until the law rounds them up and puts them where they ought to be," observed Sergeant Hal sagely. "Let's forget the fellow, Noll, unless we see him again. Tomba is evidently up to something crooked, and we're not, so we haven't any real interest in him, have we?"

"Except to be on our guard," said Noll.

"You speak as though you had some forebodings regarding Tomba, or Tomba and his friend," smiled Hal quizzically.

"Well, then, I have," returned Noll Terry.

"Not scared, are you?"

"That's a fine question to ask a soldier," sniffed Noll.

"Well, I'm not going to waste any more thoughts on Tomba, or on his white-man companion, either. Whee! Look at that rain. It——"

But a fearfully vivid flash of tropical lightning caused Sergeant Hal Overton to step further back into the little shed and close his eyes for an instant. Right after the flash came a prolonged, heavy roll of thunder that made the earth shake.

"*Cochero, para!*" shouted Noll right after that, and a fareless *quilez* stopped near the door of the shed.

"*Occupado* (occupied)?" called Noll.

"No, señor."

Hal and Noll bolted through the rain, darted into the *quilez* through the door at the rear, and plumped themselves down on the seats.

"*Sigue directio, Malate, cuartel nipa,*" ordered Hal, thus instructing the driver to go straight ahead to Malate and to take them to the nipa barracks.

The Filipino driver himself was drenched. In his thin cotton clothing the little brown man perched on the box outside, shivered until his teeth chattered. He did not propose, however, to let personal discomfort stop him from earning a fare.

Around the Walled City (Old Manila) the *quilez* carried the young soldiers. These massive walls, centuries old, enclose perhaps a square mile of city. Once past the Walled City the little vehicle glided on through pretty Ermita. Here,

11

passing along Calle Real (Royal Street), the driver turned into the straight stretch for the next suburb, Malate.

For months before sailing for the Philippines both young sergeants had devoted a good deal of their spare time to the study of Spanish. They had, however, learned the best Spanish of old Castile. First Sergeant Gray, who had put in three terms of service in the Philippines, had taken pains to teach them much of the local Spanish dialect as it is spoken in this far-away colony of Uncle Sam's.

To-day the Filipino children speak English rather well and musically, for English is the language of the public schools of the islands. Many of the older natives, however, even those with English-speaking children, know only a few words at most of the tongue of the *Americanos*.

By the time that the little cab turned in at the barracks grounds much of the fury of the storm had passed. The rain, however, continued at a steady downpour, and seemed good for the night.

"We may have to be campaigning in this kind of weather in another fortnight," remarked Hal.

"Fine business," commented Noll dryly.

"Well, it all goes in the life of a soldier. It can't hurt the soldier much, either, for somehow he's healthier than fellows who clerk or work in machine shops."

"Clerking? Shops?" repeated Noll, with a smile of mild disgust. "Did we ever stand that sort of life, Hal?"

"Once upon a time, Noll."

"Thank goodness that day has gone by."

"Here we are," announced Sergeant Hal, reaching for the rear door and opening it. "I'll pay the *cochero* this time, Noll; you paid for our last ride."

On the broad veranda of the barracks, well out of the rain, lounged half a hundred of the men of the Thirty-fourth. A few of them were at tables writing home letters.

"Did you give my regards to the Escolta, Sergeant?" called Private Kelly, from one of the groups.

"I didn't forget you, Kelly," laughed Hal.

"Get those picture post cards for me?" called Corporal Hyman.

"Here you are, Hyman," responded Noll, opening his blouse and exploring an inner pocket. "I hope I haven't got them too wet, and that the views will suit."

"Any views will suit," retorted Hyman. "My kid brothers and cousins have never been out here and one view will please them as well as another."

A few more soldiers came forward to ask about errands that the young sergeants had undertaken. No one's commissions had been forgotten.

"Your leave didn't do you two so much good this afternoon," grinned Corporal Hyman.

"Why not?" Sergeant Overton wanted to know.

"On account of the weather we didn't have parade, anyway."

"I'm no parade shirker," retorted Hal. "On the busiest day we're not being overworked here. We may strike something hard in the tropics yet, but so far, since reaching Manila, the men of this regiment haven't been worked more than a quarter as hard as in barracks at home. But I wonder when we go south?"

"Haven't you heard?" asked Corporal Hyman.

"Not a word," Hal declared.

"I haven't, either. But we heard that the 'Warren' came in this afternoon."

The "Warren" was the United States Army transport vessel that was much used in carrying troops between the different islands.

"We ought to be under way soon, then," Hal replied thoughtfully. "I suppose we're still slated to go down among the Moros."

"That's the talk in the regiment, anyway," replied Corporal Hyman.

"I hope it's true."

"You're one of the few that does, then," retorted Hyman, with a grimace. "In these islands the real fine place for a regiment to be stationed is right here on the outskirts of Manila. Plenty of grub, kitchen-cooked; little work to do, and no danger of anything except guard duty to call us out of our bunks."

"That's altogether too lazy for a soldier," objected Hal, with spirit. "I don't want to see any trouble start in these islands, but if there's going to be any campaigning, I want to see the Thirty-fourth right in the thick of it."

"You'll get over that, by and by, Sergeant," responded Corporal Hyman. "More than half of the fellows in the Thirty-fourth have been out here in other years, and have seen plenty of fighting. Now, getting shot at by a lot of strangers is all right enough for a soldier when it has to be done; but you'll find that the older men in this regiment are not doing any praying that 'Ours' will get more than its share of fighting."

"Perhaps I won't, when I've seen as much fighting as some of you fellows have," Hal nodded. "I've never been in a real battle yet."

"You've been under stiff enough fire, right back in the good old Rocky Mountains," retorted Corporal Hyman. "You don't need any more by way of training."

"Perhaps not; but I want it, just the same. I'm a hog, ain't I?" laughed the boyish young sergeant.

"No; you're simply a kid soldier," grumbled Hyman. "All the kids want a heap of fighting—until after they've had it. When you've been with the colors a few years longer you'll be ready to agree that three 'squares' a day and a soft bed at night are miles and miles ahead of desperate charges or last-ditch business."

"So the 'Warren' is in port from her last trip south," Hal went on. "Oh, I wonder when we start."

"So do a lot of us," retorted Private Kelly. "But we hope it won't be soon, Sarge."

"Oh, you coffee-coolers!" taunted Hal good-naturedly.

The Army "coffee-cooler" is the man who is left behind in stirring times. Uncle Sam's soldiers explain that a coffee-cooler is a man who won't go forward, in the morning, until his coffee is cool enough for him to drink it with comfort. Hence a coffee-cooler is a man who is detailed on work at the rear of the fighting line simply because he is of no earthly use at the front.

It is not as bad, however, to be a coffee-cooler as a cold-foot. A "cold-foot" is a soldier paralyzed with terror; he is worse than useless anywhere in the Army. The cold-foot is ironically asked why he didn't bring his woolen socks along. If a cold-foot gets into deadly action it is said that the cold chills chase each other down his spine and all settle in his feet, so that he is frozen in his tracks. However, a soldier who betrays cowardice in the face of the enemy may be shot for his cowardice, for which reason "cold feet" sometimes become cold for all time to come.

Soldiers there have been who have shown "cold feet" in their first battle or two, and yet have been among the best of soldiers later on. But the cold-foot is a rarity, anyway, among the regulars.

"Hello," broke in Kelly, peering out through the rain, "there goes some good fellow to the rainmakers."

Many of the other soldiers looked. Two hospital-corps men were carrying a stretcher in the direction of the post hospital. None could make out, however, who was on the stretcher, as, owing to the downpour of rain, the unfortunate one was covered with three or four rubber ponchos.

"I hope none of our good fellows is badly hurt," broke in Sergeant Noll Terry.

"Rheumatism, most likely," grunted Corporal Hyman. "Did you ever see a country where the rain fell as steadily when it got started?"

"Well, this is the rainy season, isn't it?" inquired Noll.

"Yes."

"But half of the year we have a dry season, don't we?"

"We do," admitted Hyman. "Yet, of the two, you'll prefer the wet season a whole lot. In the dry season the dust is blowing in your face day and night."

An orderly stepped briskly out on the veranda.

"Sergeant Overton is directed to report immediately to Lieutenant Prescott at the latter's quarters."

"I'll be there before the words are out of your mouth, Driggs," laughed Hal, rising and starting.

"Hold on, Sarge," called Private Kelly. "Look at the sheets of dew coming down, and you haven't your poncho. Here, put mine on."

"Thank you; I will," Hal assented, halting.

The poncho is a thin rubber, blanket-like affair. In the field the men usually spread the poncho on the ground, under their blankets. But in the middle of the poncho is a hole through which the head may be thrust, the poncho then falling over the trunk of the body like a rain coat.

Getting this on and replacing his campaign hat, Hal started briskly toward officers' quarters.

Lieutenant Prescott was in his room when Hal knocked, and promptly called, "Come in."

Hal entered, saluting his lieutenant, who was writing at a table. He looked up long enough to receive and return Hal's soldierly salute.

"With you in a moment, Sergeant," stated Lieutenant Prescott, who then turned back to his writing.

"Very good, sir."

14

Hal did not stir, but merely changed from his position of attention to one of greater ease.

Lieutenant Prescott is no stranger to our readers. He was second lieutenant of Captain Cortland's B Company of the Thirty-fourth. Readers of our "High School Boys Series" recall Dick Prescott as a schoolboy athlete, and readers of the "West Point Series" have followed the same Dick Prescott through his four years of cadetship at the United States Military Academy.

After finishing a page and signing it, Lieutenant Prescott wiped his pen, laid it down and wheeled about in his chair.

"You heard about Sergeant Gray?" asked the young West Pointer.

"Nothing in especial, sir."

"He was badly hurt ten minutes ago in stopping the runaway horses of Colonel Thorpe, of the Thirty-seventh Infantry. Colonel Thorpe was visiting our colonel, and only the two little Thorpe youngsters were in the carriage when the horses bolted, pitching the native driver from the seat."

"Badly hurt, sir?" cried Hal Overton in a tone of genuine distress. "That will be bad news in the company, sir. I don't think any of them know it yet, or I would have heard it before. Sergeant Gray is a man we swear by, sir, in the squad rooms."

"Sergeant Gray is a splendid soldier," observed Lieutenant Prescott warmly. "It is not believed that he will have to be retired, but he may have to put in two or three months on sick report before he can come back to duty. But that is not what I sent for you to tell you, Sergeant Overton. As Sergeant Hupner was left behind on detailed duty in the United States, the accident to Gray now leaves you the ranking sergeant in the company. Until further orders you will take over the duties of acting first sergeant, by Captain Cortland's direction."

"Very good, sir."

"This is Tuesday, Sergeant. Thursday, at eleven in the morning, the Thirty-fourth is due before the office of the captain of the port, to take boats for the transport 'Warren.' This regiment sails for Iloilo and other ports."

"May I repeat that to the men, sir?"

"It is going to be necessary, for you will have to see to it that all the personal and company baggage is ready for the teamsters at four to-morrow afternoon."

"Very good, sir."

"And, Sergeant, this is not official, but I believe it to be reliable; some of the Moro *dattos* (chieftains) are said to be preparing to stir up trouble in some of the southern islands. In that case the Thirty-fourth will bear the brunt of it all."

"I am really very glad to hear that, sir," cried Sergeant Hal eagerly.

"So am I, Sergeant," admitted the lieutenant, who, like most of the younger officers, hungered for active service against an enemy. "You understand your instructions, Sergeant?"

"Yes, sir."

"Very good; that is all, Sergeant."

Hal Overton saluted his officer with even more snap than usual, then hastened back to barracks.

Supper soon followed, and before the meal was over the rain had stopped. After supper several of B Company's men went out into the near-by street to stroll in the somewhat cooler air of the tropical evening.

A little later Hal and Noll followed. Presently, in the shadow under a densely foliaged yllang-yllang tree, they came upon two figures standing there, just in time to hear Corporal Hyman's voice saying heartily:

"That sounds like just as good a time as you make it out to be. And it won't take us over three hours? This is a hard night to get off, as the packing-up order has been given. I'll see our first sergeant, however, and find out whether there's any chance of my getting leave for the evening. If he says so, I can put it by the captain all right. Wait here, and——"

"I guess it won't be necessary, Corporal Hyman," broke in Hal's voice, sounding rather cool, for Hal had recognized Hyman's companion—none other than Vicente Tomba.

"Hello! There you are, Sarge," cried Hyman, while the little Filipino dandy started, peered at the young sergeants and then scowled.

"I'll try to fix it for you to get a pass to-night, Corporal," Hal went on, "if you really want one. But I don't exactly believe that you do. This native gentleman tried to butt in with us this afternoon, and at first we took it in good part. But he was too eager. Then, a little later in the afternoon, we heard him denouncing us to a white man because we weren't eager enough. Corporal, unless you know a lot about this man, I don't believe you want anything to do with him."

Tomba's face was blazing hotly, while his eyes gleamed angrily at Sergeant Overton's words.

"If that's the kind of fellow he is, then I don't want a pass to-night," Hyman replied. "This little man has just been telling me how much he loves American *soldados*, and he proposed to get a *quilez* and take me over into the city for the time of my life."

"From what happened this afternoon I'm a little shaky on Señor Tomba," Hal continued.

"You never saw me before!" cried Tomba, wheeling about on Hal. "Liar! Thief!"

Hal's reply was prompt, sufficient, military. He delivered a short-arm, right-hand blow that struck the native in the neck, felling him to the sidewalk.

But Tomba was up in an instant, and a knife flashed in his hands.

Hal did not flinch. He leaped upon the little brown man, getting a clinch that held the rascal powerless. Then Noll coolly took away the knife, striking the blade into the tree trunk and snapping the steel in two.

"Shall I call the guard, Sergeant, to take this little brown rat?" demanded Corporal Hyman.

"No; he isn't big enough, or man enough to bother the guard with," replied young Sergeant Overton. "I'll take care of him myself."

Whirling the Filipino around, Hal gave him a vigorous start, emphasized by a kick, and Vicente Tomba slid off into the darkness.

Malay blood is not forgiving. There were other reasons, too, why it would have been far better had Sergeant Hal turned Tomba over to the guard.

CHAPTER III
PLOTTERS TRAVEL WITH THE FLAG

From the deck of the "Warren" only distant glimpses of land, on the horizon line, were visible.

The sea to-day was without a ripple, yet, as it was not raining, the sun beat down with a heat that would have wilted most of the passengers, had it not been for the awnings stretched over every deck.

Up on the saloon deck was a mixture of the field uniforms of Army officers, the white duck or cotton of male civilian passengers, and the white dresses of the women. Most of the married officers of the Thirty-fourth had brought their families along with them, and so children played along the saloon deck, or ran down among the friendly soldiers on the spar deck. Here and there, among the women, was a Yankee schoolma'am, going to some new charge in the islands.

A number of the male cabin passengers were not Army people. Some belonged to the postals service, the islands civil service, or were planters or merchants of wealth and influence in the islands, who had been permitted to take passage on the troop ship.

Between decks the enlisted men of "Ours" were quartered and berthed by companies. Each enlisted man, by way of a bed, had a bunk whose frame was of gas pipe, to which frame was swung the canvas berth. These berths were in tiers, three high.

Away forward, in special quarters by themselves, as a sort of steerage passengers, were some two score natives of the islands who were making the journey for one reason or another. These natives, however, kept to themselves, and the soldiers saw little of them.

Altogether, the "Warren" carried something more than fourteen hundred passengers, which meant that quarters were at least sufficiently crowded. Yet the soldiers, with the cheerful good nature of their kind, took this crowded condition as one of the incidents of the life.

Noll was up on deck enjoying himself; Hal, as acting first sergeant, was otherwise occupied during the greater part of the forenoon. At the head of B Company's quarters, two decks below, young Overton sat at a little table, busily working over a set of papers that he had to make up. This "paper work" is one of the banes of first sergeants and of company commanders.

It was after eleven o'clock when Sergeant Hal finished his last sheet. The papers he folded neatly and thrust them into a long, official envelope, which he endorsed and blotted. Rising, he thrust the envelope into the breast of his blouse and started for the nearest companionway.

"I'm glad, old fellow, that you are the acting first sergeant," grinned comfortable Noll Terry, as his chum came upon deck with forehead, face and neck beaded with perspiration.

"Oh, it doesn't hurt a fellow to have a little work to do," replied Overton, smiling. "You see, you've just been loafing this morning, almost ever since inspection, while I have a consciousness of work well performed."

"Keep your consciousness and enjoy it," retorted Noll, as the two boyish sergeants stepped along the deck.

"I wonder if Captain Cortland is on deck at this moment?" remarked Sergeant Hal.

"I saw him five minutes ago," Noll answered.

Almost at that moment B Company's commander came to the forward rail of the saloon deck and looked down. Then his glance rested on Hal.

"Are the papers ready, Sergeant?" the captain called down.

"Yes, sir; I have them with me," replied Hal. Pressing through the throng of soldiers, he ascended the steps to the saloon deck, saluting and passing over the envelope.

"Thank you, Sergeant."

"I think you'll find them all right, sir. I'm somewhat new at the work, but I've taken a lot of pains."

"There's always a lot of pains taken with any work that you do, Sergeant."

"Thank you, sir."

Hal saluted and was about to turn away when he heard a voice saying:

"What we need, in dealing with the Moros in these southern islands, is to show them that——"

Just then the speaker happened to turn, and stopped talking for a moment.

The voice was new, but Sergeant Overton started at sight of the speaker's face.

"Why, that's the same big, florid-faced fellow that I saw in the shed with Tomba, that time it rained so hard," flashed through the young sergeant's astonished mind. "What can he be doing here—a cabin passenger on a United States troop ship?"

Unconsciously Hal was staring hard at the stranger. It appeared to annoy the florid-faced man.

"Well, my man," he cried impatiently, looking keenly at Hal, "are you waiting to say something to me?"

"No, sir," Sergeant Hal replied quickly.

"Perhaps you thought you knew me?"

"No, sir; I merely remembered having once seen you."

"You've seen me before? Then your memory is better than mine, Sergeant. Where have you ever seen me before?"

"The other afternoon, sir, on the south side of the Pasig River at Manila. You were in a shed, out of the rain, with a native calling himself Vicente Tomba."

The florid-faced man betrayed neither uneasiness nor resentment. Instead, he smiled pleasantly as he replied:

"I thought you were in error, Sergeant, and now I'm certain of it, for I don't know any Vicente Tomba."

"Then I beg your pardon for the mistake, sir," Hal replied quickly.

"No need to apologize, Sergeant, for you have done no harm," replied the florid-faced man.

Here Captain Cortland's voice broke in, cool and steady:

"Yet I know, Mr. Draney, that Sergeant Overton feels embarrassed by the mere fact of his having made a mistake. Sergeant Overton is one of our best and most capable soldiers, and he rarely makes a mistake of any kind."

"I'm glad to hear that he's one of your best soldiers," replied Draney pleasantly. "It seems odd, doesn't it, Captain, to see so boyish a chap wearing sergeant's chevrons?"

"Sergeant Overton, Mr. Draney, is more than merely a sergeant. He is acting first sergeant of B Company, and is likely to continue as such for some months to come."

"He has risen so high?" cried Draney. "I certainly congratulate the young man."

There appeared to be no further call for Hal to remain on the saloon deck. After flashing an inquiring look at his company commander, and saluting that officer, Hal next raised his uniform cap to Draney, then turned and made his way down to the spar deck.

"Your sergeant looks like a very upright young man, Captain," observed Mr. Draney.

"Overton?" rejoined Captain Cortland. "I am certain that he is the soul of honor."

"His loyalty has often been tested, I presume?" persisted the florid-faced fellow.

"He's a very thoroughly trustworthy young man, if that's what you mean."

Captain Cortland was beginning to feel somewhat annoyed, for, truth to tell, he did not like Draney very well.

"Is your sergeant," asked Draney, "a young man much interested in the joys of life, or is he of the quiet, studious sort who seldom care for good times?"

"You seem to be uncommonly interested in Sergeant Overton, Mr. Draney," remarked the captain almost testily.

"Only as a type of American soldier," replied Draney blandly. "I was wondering if my estimate of the young man were borne out by your experience with him."

"Sergeant Overton is fond of the joys of life, if you mean the quiet and decent pleasures. He is a good deal of a student, and that type is never interested in drinking or gambling, or any of the vices and dissipations, if that is what you mean."

Then, noting that Colonel North had just stepped out on deck from his stateroom, Captain Cortland added hastily:

"Pardon me; I wish to speak with the commanding officer."

As colonel and captain met they exchanged salutes.

"I told Draney, sir, that I wished to speak with you," Captain Cortland reported, in a low voice. "I did not tell him, however, that I wished to speak with you mainly as a pretext for getting away from his society."

"You don't like Draney?" smiled Colonel North, eying his captain shrewdly.

"I certainly do not," Cortland confessed.

"And I'm almost as certain that I don't, either," replied the regimental commander. "However, Cortland, we shall have to treat him with a fair amount

19

of courtesy, for Draney is an influential man down in the part of the world for which we are headed. He is influential with the Moros, I mean. Often he is in a position to give the military authorities useful information of intended native mischief. Draney is a very big planter, you know, and white planters are somewhat scarce in the Moro country. It is one of the great disappointments of our government that more American capital is not invested in establishing great plantations in the extremely rich Moro country. But, as you know, Cortland, some of the Moro dattos are given to heading sudden, unexpected and very desperate raids on white planters, and that fact has discouraged Americans, Englishmen and Germans from investing millions and millions of capital in the Moro country."

"Yet the fellow Draney is a planter there, sir?"

"Draney owns half a dozen very successful plantations."

"And is he never molested by the Moros, sir?" inquired Captain Cortland.

"Never enough to discourage him in his investments. Rather odd, isn't it, Cortland?"

"Very odd, indeed, sir," replied Captain Cortland dryly.

That same afternoon Captain Cortland, after finishing a promenade on the saloon deck, went forward, descending to the spar deck. There, under the awning, he came upon Sergeants Hal and Noll, who saluted as he addressed them.

"Sergeant Overton," began the captain in a low tone, "you seemed, this forenoon, to feel a good deal of surprise at seeing Mr. Draney on board."

"I was surprised, sir."

"Tell me what you know about the man."

Sergeant Hal briefly related the adventure that he and Noll had had with Vicente Tomba on the Escolta, and their subsequent meeting with Tomba and Draney on the south side of the Pasig. Hal also repeated what they had overheard Tomba saying to Draney. Hal then described the flight of the pair in the *quilez*.

"Yet Draney declares that he never heard of Tomba," said the captain musingly. "Sergeant Overton, do you think it possible that you have mistaken Mr. Draney for someone else?"

"It may be, of course, sir," Hal admitted. "But I hardly believe it possible. Besides, I have pointed out Mr. Draney to Sergeant Terry and he also is positive that it is the same man."

At that moment all three turned to look forward. There was some sort of commotion going on there. It proved, however, to be nothing but the herding of the Filipino passengers on deck near the bow, while one of the regiment's officers was inspecting their quarters below.

The three officers returned to their conversation, but presently Hal murmured:

"Don't look immediately, Noll, but presently take a passing glance at the Filipino standing away up in the bow. Tell Captain Cortland who the fellow is."

"It's Vicente Tomba, although I'd hardly know him in that costume of the *peon* (laborer)," Noll answered.

"You are both certain that the man is Tomba?" inquired Captain Cortland keenly.

"Yes, sir," both young sergeants declared, and Hal added:

"There's Corporal Hyman up forward, sir. If you'll go up and speak to the corporal, and allow us to accompany you, sir, you can see whether Hyman knows the fellow. He, too, was approached by Tomba, at the nipa barracks."

Accordingly the test was made.

"Why, certainly, the fellow is Tomba," replied Hyman, "though he looks a lot different, sir, from the dandy who was talking to me last Tuesday night."

Captain Cortland asked all three of the non-commissioned officers some further questions as they stood there. None of the quartette discovered the fact that, close to them, crouching under the canvas cover of a life boat as it swung at davits, lay one of the keen-eyed Filipino passengers. This swarthy little fellow was only about half versed in English, but he understood enough of the talk to realize what was in the wind.

In some mysterious manner what this swarthy little spy overheard traveled, less than an hour later, to Mr. Draney, planter, and that gentleman, as he sat in his stateroom and thought it all over, was greatly disturbed.

Still later that afternoon—not long before sundown—while the "Warren" was still ploughing her way through the sea, the little brown spy drew Vicente Tomba to one side in the native steerage.

To make assurance doubly sure, both Filipinos spoke in their own Malay dialect, the Tagalos.

"Tomba!"

"Luis?"

"Tomba, the Señor Draney is greatly disturbed. Sergeant Overton and Sergeant Terry have recognized him as one whom they saw with you in Manila."

"Bah! That amounts to little. Señor Draney can deny."

"But they have recognized you also, my Tomba, and so has Corporal Hyman. More, they have told Captain Cortland all they know, and all they can guess."

"The dogs!" growled Vicente Tomba, his snarl showing his fine, white teeth.

"You do well to call them dogs," grinned Luis. "Señor Draney bids me to remind you what becomes of dogs that are troublesome. You have others here with you who can help. At the first chance, then, Overton, Terry and Hyman are to bite the bone that kills—and Captain Cortland, too, if you can manage it!"

CHAPTER IV

CERVERRA'S INNOCENT SHOP

"D'ye know what I'm thinking about?" demanded Private Kelly, as he turned to look out southward from Fort Benjamin Franklin.

"Not being a mind reader—no," replied Hal.

"I'm thinking this country is a fine place to dream about."

"It's worth it," declared Sergeant Overton, with unsullied boyish enthusiasm.

"Worth it—huh!" retorted Kelly, who had served longer in the Army. "Mind ye, I said this was a good country to dream about. But to live in—give me 'God's country.'"

The United States soldier on foreign service, invariably alludes to home in this way.

Send him to the fairest spot on which the human eye ever rested, and the soldier will still longingly speak of home as "God's country."

"Then I'll be polite," retorted Sergeant Hal, "and say that I wish, Kelly, that you could be at home. But as for me, I'm glad I'm here."

"Wait until you are in your third enlistment, and have put in another two years in the islands, after this time," growled Kelly.

"Why, where can you find a more beautiful spot than this?" demanded Hal Overton, gazing across the fields toward the town of Bantoc. "I never saw a more beautiful spot. I wonder if there are many like it in the tropics?"

"Beautiful?" rumbled Kelly. "Sure! But ye can't eat beauty. 'Tis a long way from anywhere, this spot, and that's what I've got against it."

"Grumbling again, Kelly?" asked Sergeant Noll Terry, joining them.

"Not grumbling," retorted Kelly. "Just giving my opinion. But this boy sergeant is trying to make me think this swamp on northern Mindanao is an earthly paradise."

"Well, isn't it?" challenged Noll. "I know what ails you, Kelly. When all is peace and comfort, with three 'squares' a day, and not a heap to do, your old soldier is always kicking. But just send you and the rest, Kelly, hiking up through those mountains yonder, give you twenty miles a day of rough climbing, drown you out with rain and let you use up your shoes chasing a lot of ugly brown men, and never a kick will we hear coming from you."

"Sure, no," replied Kelly philosophically. "'Tis then we'd be doing a soldier's work, and a kicker on a hike is as useless as a coffee-cooler at an afternoon tea."

"In other words," laughed Hal, "a real soldier of the Regular Army is as patient as a camel when things are all going wrong. The only time when your real soldier kicks is when he's having it easy and is too comfortable to be patient. Curious, isn't it?"

"Oh, well, 'tis no use talking to you two," retorted Private Kelly, shaking his head and strolling away. "Ye've not seen much of service yet."

"That's another joke," laughed Hal in a low voice, as soon as Kelly had stepped out of hearing. "Here's a man like Kelly, with fairly long service to his credit, but he's a private still, and probably always will be. If the colonel made him a corporal, Kelly wouldn't rest until he had the chevrons taken from his sleeve so that he could be a private soldier again. Now you and I, Noll, work like blazes all the time, and win our promotion, yet Kelly considers us only boys, and boys who don't know much, either. Either one of us can take Kelly out in a squad and work him until he runs rivers of perspiration, and he can't talk back without danger of being disciplined. Yet all the time, Kelly, under our orders, is thinking of us, half contemptuously, as boys who don't really know anything about soldiering."

"That's because we're young," laughed Noll.

"And because we're also boyish enough to have a little enthusiasm left in our make-ups. Noll, how do you really like our new station?"

22

"I wouldn't be anywhere else," retorted Sergeant Terry, "except some where else in the Philippines, possibly. One of the prospects that caught me for the service was the chance of seeing some of our foreign possessions."

"It's what catches half the young fellows who enlist to-day," went on Hal. "I've been looking forward to the Philippines from the day I first took the oath in the recruiting station."

"Well, we're here," replied Noll, breathing in the warm air with lazy satisfaction. "And I'm mighty glad that we're in for two years of it."

The Thirty-fourth had come out to the islands as a complete regiment. They had reëmbarked at Manila also as a regiment, but now the time had come when "Ours" was well scattered through the southern islands of the archipelago.

The second battalion and headquarters, with the band, had disembarked at Iloilo; two companies had been left on the island of Negros, and two more on Cebu. B and C Companies had been left at Fort Franklin, in the Misamis district on northern Mindanao, and the remaining two companies had been carried on to Zamboanga.

On its return trip the "Warren" had picked up the scattered military commands which the Thirty-fourth had relieved. Two companies of the Thirty-second infantry had gone from Bantoc the day before.

Mindanao is the second largest and the most fertile island in the Philippine group. The natural beauty is as great as the fertility. If it were not for the occasional ferocity of some of the tribes this island could be turned into one vast net-work of plantations as rich as any that the world can show.

Bantoc was a sleepy, sunlit little town, half Spanish and half Moro. Thanks to American rule, the streets were clean and order reigned. There were about forty stores and other mercantile establishments in Bantoc, for this town was headquarters for a large country district. The people of Bantoc, outside of the small white population, were more than half Moros, the other islanders belonging to the Tagalo and other allied tribes. Almost without exception these people were lazy and good-natured. A newcomer would have difficulty in believing that such men as he met in Bantoc could ever give the soldiers trouble. It was to this town that the few planters and many small native farmers sent rich stores of rice, cocoa, hemp, cotton, indigo and costly woods.

There was also the port of Bantoc, through which these products were sent out to do their part in the world's commerce.

The native leaders of the population of Bantoc were wealthy little brown men. There was much money in circulation, the leading Moros and Tagalos having handsome homes and entertaining lavishly. There was a native fashionable set, just as exclusive and autocratic as any that exists in a white man's country.

Fort Franklin overlooked the bay at the opposite end from the port. Yet it was a "fort" only in being a military station. There was no artillery here, and the only fortifications were semi-permanent earthworks, fronted by ditches, thrown up around the officers' quarters and the barracks and other buildings. The parade ground and recreation spaces were outside these very ordinary fortifications.

"The whole scene looks too peacefully lazy to match with the yarns we hear of trouble breeding among the Moros in those mountains yonder," remarked Hal musingly.

"If trouble is coming, I hope it will come soon," returned Sergeant Noll. "The only one thing that I have against our life out here is that it threatens to become too lazy an existence. If there's going to be any active service for us, I want to see it happen soon, for active service is what I came to the Philippines for, anyway, as far as I had any interest in the trip."

"From the gossip of the town and barracks, I think we'll have our trouble soon enough," Hal replied. "You have fatigue duty this afternoon, haven't you, Noll?"

"Yes; thanks to your detail," replied Noll.

"But I couldn't help the detail, old fellow. Fatigue was for you in your turn. I'm sorry it came to you to-day, though, for I've a pass and I'm going to run over into Bantoc. I want to see more of that queer little town."

"Going to be back for parade?"

"Yes; my pass extends only to parade. I never want to miss that when I can help it."

Hal glanced at his watch, then back at barracks, where hardly a soldier showed himself, for all had caught the spirit of indolence in this hot, moist climate of Mindanao.

"Well, I must be going, Noll. Don't work your fatigue party too hard until the men get used to this heat."

"Small danger of my working 'em too hard," laughed Noll. "It's only as a sort of special favor that the fellows will work at all."

Hal, with a nod to his chum, stepped out on to the hard, level, white road that led from Fort Franklin to Bantoc.

It was a pretty road, shaded at points by beautiful palms; yet the shade was not sufficient to protect the young soldier all the way into town. Ere he had gone far he found it necessary to carry his damp handkerchief in one hand, prepared to mop his steaming face.

"Mindanao is certainly some hot," he muttered. "It keeps a fellow steaming all the time."

Yet there was plenty to divert one's thoughts from himself, for along this road lay some of the prettiest small farms to be found on northern Mindanao. Instead of farms they really looked more like well-kept gardens.

"It's the finest spot in the world to be lazy in," thought the young sergeant, as he glanced here and there over the charming scene. "If I settled down here for life I'd want money enough to pay other fellows to do all the work for me."

Though Hal did not know it, from the window of one room in a house that he passed a pair of unusually bright, keen eyes glared out at him.

"That is he, the *sergente*, Overton," growled Vicente Tomba to himself. "Since we have Señor Draney's orders that the *sergente* is to leave this life as soon as possible, why not to-day? He is going to Bantoc, where it will be easy to snare him. And his friend Terry is not with him. That pair, back to back, might put up a hard fight—but one alone should be easy for our *bravos*. Then, another day, we can plan to get the *Sergente* Terry."

24

Hal was not quite in Bantoc when a Tagalo on a pony rode by him at a gallop. Hal glanced at the fellow indolently, but did not recognize him, as it was not Tomba, but one of that worthy's messengers.

Up and down the principal street Sergeant Overton wandered. He glanced into shops, though only idly, for to-day he was not on a buying mission.

At last the cool-looking interior of a little restaurant attracted him. He entered, ordering an ice cream. When this was finished he ate another. It was so restful, sitting here, that when he had disposed of the second order, he paid his account but did not rise at once.

"The *sergente* is newly arrived here?" asked a white-clad Filipino, rising from another table and joining Overton.

"Yes."

"Then you have not seen much of Bantoc?" asked the Filipino, speaking in Spanish.

"Not as much as I mean to see of the town," Hal answered in the same tongue.

"Then possibly, Señor Sergente, you have not yet seen the collection of ancient Moro weapons in the shop of Juan Cerverra."

"I haven't," Hal admitted.

"Then you have missed much, señor, but you will no doubt go to see the collection one of these days."

"I'd like to. Where is the shop?"

"Four doors below here. If you have time, Señor Sergente, I am walking that way and will show you the place."

"Thank you; I'll be glad to go," answered Hal, rising promptly. His was the profession of arms, and a display of any unfamiliar weapons was sure to attract the young sergeant.

Juan Cerverra, despite his Spanish-sounding name, proved to be a full-blooded Moro. He wore his Moro costume, with its tight-fitting trousers and short, embroidered blouse. There were no customers in the shop when Hal and his Tagalo acquaintance entered.

In another moment Sergeant Hal was deeply absorbed in several wall cases of swords and knives, all of them of old-time patterns. It was a sight that would have bewildered a lover and collector of curios of past ages.

One case was filled entirely with fine specimens of that once-dreaded weapon, the Moro "campilan." This is a straight sword, usually, with a very heavy blade, which gradually widens towards the end. This is a heavy cutting sword, and one that was placed in Sergeant Hal's hands, though Cerverra claimed that it was two hundred years old, had an edge like a razor.

"How much is such a sword as this?" Hal inquired.

"Forty dollars," replied Cerverra.

"Gold!"

"No; Mex."

Hal felt almost staggered with the cheapness of things here, as compared with the curio stores in Manila. Forty dollars "Mex" meant but about twenty dollars in United States currency.

"I have some cheaper ones," went on Cerverra. "Here is one at eighteen dollars."

"I'm going to have one of these campilan," Hal told himself.

In his interest he did not note that the Tagalo who had brought him to the shop had left him and was standing on the sidewalk outside.

"Are you interested in these creeses?" inquired Cerverra, passing down the shop and pointing to another wall case.

The creese is an ancient Malay knife, with a waved, snaky blade—a weapon with which the Malay pirates of the past used to do fearful execution.

Hal stepped before the wall case. "They are very interesting looking," he replied. "What does a good creese cost?"

The young sergeant did not wait for an answer.

Click! A spring bolt on the under side of a trap door on which he was standing shot out of place.

Down dropped the trap door with such suddenness that Hal Overton did not have even time to clutch at anything.

Then the trap door, relieved of his weight, flew back into place.

Sergeant Hal shot down a steep incline, too smooth for him to be able to stay his downward progress.

CHAPTER V
ENOUGH TO "RATTLE" THE VICTIM

Bump!

Sergeant Hal landed at least twenty feet below with a suddenness that jarred all the breath out of him for a moment.

Ere he could recover his half-scattered senses he felt himself seized. Nor had the Army boy fallen into one pair of hands. Four or five men, as nearly as he could judge, seized hold of different parts of his body.

There was little use in a prostrate youth fighting against such odds. Hal was swiftly rolled over on to his face, in the dark, and two of his captors threw themselves upon him, holding him down.

At the same time another thrust an armful of hemp under his face, holding it close against his mouth.

Then the light of a dark lantern was flashed on the scene. With the speed of skilled hands at the game these brown-skinned captors bound the young sergeant hand and foot.

"Quit this!" Sergeant Overton tried to shout angrily, but the wad of hemp was forced between his teeth and only a faint sound came forth.

"Help!" he tried to shout, but the sound came hardly louder than a sigh.

Now he was whirled over on his back, helpless, and two of the brown rascals finished their work by thrusting the hemp far enough into his mouth to shut off all speech. Then the gag was bound into place.

Hal could form little idea of his prison, save that it was an oblong, cellar-like place, perhaps a dozen feet wide by twenty feet long.

As nearly as the Army boy could guess, this cellar must be located under the street itself.

"They've got me for fair," thought the young soldier in a rage that included himself as well as his captors. "What's their game, I wonder? Robbery? If it is, they'll feel sold when they find how little money they are going to get."

By the light of the dark lantern, as he lay on his back on the damp ground, Hal made out the fact that his captors numbered eight. Five men had the look and wore the costumes of Moros; the other three rascals looked as though they might be Tagalos.

One after another the wretches looked down at the young soldier and grinned, though not one of them spoke.

Of a sudden the light went out. Hal, his ears unusually acute now, heard their moving footsteps. Then all became intensely still.

"I wonder whether I'm a tremendously big fool, or whether I'm merely unfortunate?" thought Hal bitterly. "However, how was I to guess? In this Moro country must it be considered unsafe even to step into a store and look at the merchandise?"

There was no answer to this. By degrees Hal began to feel decidedly uncomfortable as to the fate that he might expect.

"If they meant only to rob me," he reflected, "then why didn't they proceed at once? But not a single brown rascal of the lot took the trouble to thrust an exploring hand into my pockets. What, then? Do they want an Army prisoner, and if so, for what?"

The longer the young soldier thought it over, the greater the puzzle became. Nor did it escape his imagination that possibly he was not to be allowed ever to see his comrades again. That thought, of course, sent a chill of horror chasing up and down young Overton's spine. He was not afraid to die in battle, if need be— but to be treated like a rat in a trap—that was different.

"Well, they've got me, and I don't see any likelihood of getting away," decided Hal at last, after fully an hour devoted largely to futile efforts to wriggle out of the bonds that held his wrists secure behind his back. "These knots have been tied by masters. I don't believe I could get out of them in hours. If they had only tied my hands in front of me, so that I could work them loose. Confound the pirates!"

After what seemed like the passage of hours, the boy heard a slight sound. Listening intently, he heard it repeated.

Next a light was turned on—from the same dark lantern.

Behind the light Hal's dazzled eyes could make out the figure of a man.

Toward him the light came, Hal blinking in the glare until the newcomer halted beside him.

"Ah, Señor Sergente!" cried a mocking voice.

Then the new comer bent over the Army boy, and Overton knew him in an instant—Vicente Tomba.

"That hemp in your mouth looks as though it might give you discomfort—a thousand pardons," observed Tomba mockingly, as he removed the cord that held the hemp in place.

Tomba now squatted on the ground beside the young soldier's head and drew out the wad of hemp.

"So you are in this, Tomba?" inquired the Army boy coldly. "What's the game, anyway?"

"Possibly," sneered the Filipino, "when you know more, you'll feel like making a noise. Let me assure you that no friend will hear if you do call. But any great amount of noise on your part might provoke me, and that would not be wise under the circumstances."

Showing his white, even teeth in an evil smile, Tomba took out of the breast of his blouse a small, bright-bladed creese that might have been borrowed from one of the wall cases in Cerverra's shop.

"Why has this trick been played on me?" demanded Sergeant Hal angrily.

"A trick?" laughed Tomba softly. "Is that what you think it is? My friend, you will find that it is much more than a trick—it is a decree!"

"A decree?" raged Sergeant Overton. "What do you mean?"

"It is a decree from Señor Draney," went on Tomba coldly, maliciously. "It can do no harm to mention that name since you can never repeat it to anyone but me, for Señor Draney's decree is that, when you go forth from here—to-night— you will know nothing afterwards, for you will be *past knowing*."

CHAPTER VI
LIFE HANGS ON A WORD

"You are talking like a madman," sneered Hal.

"And next you will be begging like one," returned Tomba, with that same easy but deadly laugh.

Hal, despite his grit, felt a start of terror. Cold sweat was now gathering on his forehead.

"You refused my friendship some days ago," continued Tomba. "You did not know how valuable it might be."

"Can the friendship of a scoundrel like you ever be valuable?" asked Overton.

"In the present case it would be worth a little to you—your life!"

"What did you want of me, when you sought my acquaintance?" demanded Hal.

He had suddenly become seized with a desire to prolong the talk with this little brown monster—to gain time!

"There was something that you could have done for me," replied Vicente Tomba.

The Tagalo, like others of his race, was not averse to talking, either. The little Filipino knew that he had the whole situation in his hands. With the cruelty of a cat, Tomba delighted in the feline pastime of playing with a victim that could not escape him.

"What did you want me to do?" Hal asked almost blandly.

"I wanted your services."

"Yes, but what kind of services?"

"What is the use of telling you—*now*?"

"Tell me one thing, though, Tomba."

"Why?"

28

"Just to gratify my curiosity," explained Sergeant Hal, and he spoke slowly while his eyes watched those of the Filipino. "Did you want me to betray my Flag?"

"Not the Flag itself."

"But, in some way, you wanted me to turn against my comrades—to serve you and your friends at the expense of the United States Government."

"Yes," assented Tomba. "But do not think to deceive me. It is too late now to save yourself by promising what I would have wanted of you."

"I don't intend to serve you and your rascal friends at any price—at least, I haven't yet come to that decision," Hal added, in a more conciliatory tone. "However, I am curious."

"Curiosity can do you no good now," retorted Tomba softly, with a shrug of his shoulders.

"What part is Draney playing with you brown-skinned men?"

Tomba again shrugged his shoulders, this time more mockingly.

"Señor Draney serves the same cause that I do," laughed the Filipino.

"And what cause is that?"

"His purse."

"Then, in other words, Tomba, you are not even a Filipino patriot. You are merely a twentieth-century type of pirate."

"If you like the word," replied Tomba, in a tone of indifference.

Then he yawned—next placed the creese on the ground beside him, while his right hand explored his pockets. He soon brought to light a package of Manila cigarettes. Tomba's left hand produced a box of matches.

"Do you care for one last smoke, Señor Sergente?" inquired the Filipino with mocking politeness, as he held out the package.

"Thank you; I never picked up the vice," Sergeant Hal answered, but he said it good-naturedly, for he had an object now in not provoking the enemy.

"So? You call smoking a vice?"

"The vice of pigs," declared Hal, but again he laughed good-humoredly.

"Oh, I do not mind your insolence," replied Tomba, striking a match and holding it to the end of the cigarette in his mouth. "Abuse me all you please, Señor Sergente."

"Thank you!"

Hal had had a desperate motive in gaining time by prolonging the talk. As he lay on his side before the Filipino the young soldier had at last employed his fingers in a way that he hoped would lead to his being able to free his hands. And now the instant had come! His hands were free!

As he uttered that "thank you," Sergeant Overton suddenly summoned all the muscles in his body to obey him in one frantic effort for safety and freedom.

Like a flash he rolled, both of his bound feet kicking Vicente Tomba and bowling over that astounded little brown man.

Like lightning the Army boy reached for the creese, and the finish of that general movement found Sergeant Hal Overton sitting up and aiming a desperate slash at the cord about his ankles.

It needed a second slash, and in that fleeting interval Vicente Tomba, uttering a wild cry of rage, hurled himself upon the Army boy.

Hal Overton had now, however, entire control of his body. He engaged with the little brown man in a desperate struggle. Over and over they rolled, the Army boy controlling the battle and carrying them both further from the creese that he had dropped on the ground.

Then, all in an instant, Hal freed his right hand, clenched his fist and struck Tomba a staggering blow between the eyes.

When Tomba came to himself again, after a few moments, he found the youth in Uncle Sam's Army uniform leaning over him.

"I have the creese, Tomba," warned Overton. "You can guess what a sound or a move that is not permitted will mean to you!"

To do his courage full justice, Tomba showed himself no coward.

"You have the upper hand, Señor Sergente. But it will do you no good."

"No?" questioned Uncle Sam's young soldier. "Why not?"

"There is but one way out of here."

"And then?"

"To pass out that way you must go by a dozen of my men, and you can judge for yourself what that will mean."

"Yes; I have an idea," nodded Hal thoughtfully.

"Then you see the folly of thinking you can escape?"

"No; I am thinking that your men will be able to get me."

"To be sure."

"Yet I am quick, Tomba, and before they can finish me, I shall have settled my score with you for good and all."

"And thrown away your own life?"

"You forget that I am a soldier, Tomba. I am inclined to feel that it will be worth even my own life to make sure that you are where you can no longer plot against the American Government."

"But your own life, Señor Sergente?"

"My own life is less than worthless to me if I may be permitted to lose it in doing one last valuable act for the Flag of my country."

"You are boasting now!"

"As to that, Tomba, you will soon be in a position to know. And I warn you that the slightest sign of treachery on your part will be my excuse for ridding these islands of the disgrace of your presence."

"You are attempting too much," jeered the little brown man. "I see and I admit that you are brave, yet you are bound to lose."

"The time for talking is past, Tomba, and now we come to action," returned the Army boy, speaking slowly and easily. "Come, get upon your feet and obey every order of mine the instant that you receive it. In another minute or two you and I will be in the sunlight again—or else you and I have both already had our last glimpse of the light of day.

Tomba smiled, though he felt the mastery of this young wearer of Uncle Sam's uniform.

"Get up on your feet," ordered Hal. "Stand right before me, your back to me. Do you feel the point of the creese?"

"Yes," answered Tomba in a low voice, though the brown man spoke steadily.

"You will walk before me, very slowly. If you attempt to turn, or to disobey, I shall know what to do with this wavy-bladed creese. If you make a move to spring away from me, I shall show you how good a jumper I am—and then the creese! Now, walk, very slowly, toward the exit from this place."

Steady, Now, Tomba!

As they started Hal held the lantern with his left hand so that the rays of light flashed ahead of them.

Vicente Tomba walked to the far end of this underground room. As far as young Overton's eyes could see they were moving toward a blank wall.

"Halt!" commanded the young sergeant easily.

Tomba obeyed.

"You are taking me to a secret door?"

"It is so, señor."

"And you know how to open it?"

"Yes; it is simple."

"Then step to the door. But, Tomba!"

31

"Si, señor."

"Do not let any wild plan run through your mind that you will open the door suddenly, bolt through it and close it in my face. Do you still feel the creese? Well, I am on the alert!"

In truth that had been Vicente Tomba's very plan. Now he gave up the idea, for Sergeant Hal's tone and manner made it very plain that treachery would prove but another name for suicide.

"Then look out, Señor Sergente, that when I open the door there is no rush on the part of my brave ones."

"Whether you or they plan the rush, it will be the end of the world for you, Tomba," Overton warned him steadily.

"I will do my best, señor," replied Tomba in a voice well nigh as steady as the Army boy's.

Then he bent forward, pressing until he found a hidden spring. In the seemingly solid stone wall a large block of stone swung around on a pivot, disclosing a larger cellar room beyond.

"Steady, now, Tomba!"

Sergeant Overton flashed the lantern's rays over the Filipino's left shoulder.

Nor was it a reassuring sight that the light of the lantern revealed to the young soldier.

Instead of a dozen brown-skinned men in the next room, there were eight, if Hal's hurried count was correct. Moreover, he believed them to be the same eight who had first received and bound him.

The most disquieting fact, however, was that five of the men wore revolvers at their belts, and a pistol usually has a knife at a disadvantage.

"Explain to them, Tomba," muttered the young soldier in English, "that any move of your own, or any move of theirs to help you, will be expensive for you. Warn them, for I am watching all the rascals at once and I shall not endure an instant's treachery or disobedience of my orders."

Tomba spoke to them rapidly, partly in the Tagalo and partly in the Moro dialect. Sergeant Hal listened, watched, waited in keen anxiety, for life and death hung on the issue.

CHAPTER VII

THE KIND OF MAN WHO MASTERS OTHERS

Every one of the eight sullen fellows stood as though rooted in his tracks.

While Tomba spoke none answered, but many baleful glances were cast at Sergeant Hal Overton of the Thirty-fourth Infantry.

When Tomba had ceased speaking two or three of the rascals spoke, slowly, briefly.

"What do the scoundrels say?" demanded the Army boy.

"They do not like the situation, señor."

"Can you blame them? Or can they help the situation in the new turn that it has taken?"

The Filipino shrugged his shoulders.

"Well, ask the brown pirates what they intend to do?"

Tomba spoke as though translating the question into the two tongues that these surly fellows understood.

"They say that they do not know," replied Vicente Tomba presently.

"Can't make up their minds, eh?" jeered Hal. "Then I'll form their decisions for them. There's a further way out of this place?"

Vicente Tomba hesitated, muttering.

"Now, don't you try my old trick of trying to gain time," warned the boyish sergeant crisply. "I know all about that little trick and I don't intend to put up with it in the enemy. Tomba, tell your fellows to open the way out of here, and to get out as quickly as they know how. Tell them that, as soon as you stop talking, I'm going to begin to count ten in English, and that the instant I count ten I shall drive this creese deep into the back of your neck. Tell them that I know how to handle a weapon like this, and that I'll finish you with one blow."

As he spoke, Sergeant Hal dropped the lantern that he had been holding with his left hand. It fell with a crash, and the light went out, but he needed it no longer, for there were two other lighted lanterns in the room.

"Go on, Tomba! Tell them just what I told you to say. Be sure you get it straight, too. Remember how much hangs in the balance for you!"

Tomba began speaking, his voice wonderfully steady. Sergeant Hal could not help admiring the evident courage of this little Filipino, who knew well enough that his life was hanging on a thread from second to second.

Hal's left hand now rested tightly on the little brown man's shoulder. Tomba's body was no slight protection against the pistols of these surly fellows in case they evidenced a disposition to shoot. And the Army boy did not intend to let this human bulwark get away from him.

"You have told them, Tomba?" queried Hal Overton, as soon as the Filipino's voice ceased.

"Even so, señor."

"They understand?"

"If they do not, then they are idiots, Señor Sergente."

"Then tell them I am going to begin to count."

Again Tomba spoke, this time briefly.

The grip of young Overton's hand on the Filipino's shoulder tightened. A slight shudder ran through the brown man's frame, but otherwise he showed no fear.

"One!" began Hal.

From the surly ones beyond an angry babel of protest went up.

But Hal coolly disregarding the clamor, merely raised his own voice enough to make it heard:

"Two!"

Sergeant Overton now let go of the Filipino's shoulder, but only to throw his arm around the fellow's neck. Tomba's head was drawn back, almost chokingly, against the boyish sergeant's shoulder.

"Three!"

Still no motion among the dark-skinned eight.

"Four!"

And then:

"Five! Tomba, your friends are cheerful about your fate, aren't they? Six!"

Vicente Tomba spoke, sharply, hissingly. Now some stir was noticeable among the wretches, though whether they meant to obey or to try to rush the lone soldier was more than Overton could guess.

"Seven!"

Hal's voice, as steady as ever, must have carried conviction with it. Certainly Tomba's shuddering had increased, though the little brown man, no match in muscle for the white soldier, made not the least effort to wrest himself away from that dangerous grip.

"Eight!" announced Hal Overton, his voice on the verge of absolute cheeriness.

Again Tomba spoke, this time still more angrily.

There was a shuffling of feet, as the men moved further away. Then one of the wretches stepped forward and threw open a door, just as Hal came calmly out with:

"Nine!"

"Stop counting, señor," urged Vicente Tomba quite coolly. "These men have yielded and are going. They will open the other door, pass through it hurriedly, and leave the way open for you."

"Lucky for you, if they do, my Tagalo friend! I will suspend the count for an instant only."

Another stone door was suddenly swung open, by one of the surly fellows, revealing a passage beyond. Into this the eight fairly raced.

"Do not follow too quickly, señor, or one of the rascals may forget himself and turn to fight," declared Tomba.

"It will be bad for you if it happens!"

"It is of myself that I am thinking, señor!" returned the Filipino dryly. Then, after a pause:

"Come, señor. Surely we can pass out safely now."

"Then we'll do so," agreed Sergeant Hal, "and your life be upon our success! Don't try to go more quickly than I move, or I shall suspect you, and with me to suspect is to——"

"Say no more, señor," interrupted the little Filipino. "I understand you better than I did, and I am taking no chances."

Sergeant Overton still retained his left-handed hold on Tomba as the pair passed out to what might mean safety.

Through this second doorway they passed, to find themselves ascending a slope paved only with tightly packed dirt. Glancing up the slope Sergeant Hal made out three or four stars low down in the sky beyond.

"Night time?" he queried in mild astonishment.

"Yes, señor, and you will even believe that it is the night of another day," laughed Vicente Tomba, "for you must have lived ages in the last few hours."

"It wasn't quite as bad as that," the Army boy returned graciously. "In your way, Tomba, you helped excellently to pass the time for me."

At the top of this interior slope the pair passed out through a doorway ordinarily closed by means of a stout wooden door. The pair found themselves in the yard back of Cerverra's house. At one side was an alley way leading to the street.

"I will leave you here, señor, with your gracious permission."

"Oh, no, no, Tomba! You will go with me, and still held by me, at least as far as the middle of the street."

With sullen assent the Filipino consented to this. On their way through the alley they encountered no one.

But, just as they reached the sidewalk, they were met with a sharp hail of: "Halt!"

CHAPTER VIII
THE RIGHT MAN IN THE GUARD HOUSE

That command, however, in a good, strong American voice, had very far from the effect of startling Hal Overton.

Down the street, barely a hundred feet away, a squad of a dozen soldiers of B Company had just halted in column of twos.

At the head of the squad stood Sergeant Terry and Corporal Hyman.

"Sergeant Terry," called the self-rescued Army boy briskly, "march your men here and halt them again."

"Very good, Sergeant Overton," answered Noll's voice, precise and formal as though on parade, but there was a note of joy, none the less, in Terry's voice.

"I will go now, señor," suggested Vicente Tomba, struggling slightly to free himself as the squad again halted close to the Army boy.

"You will do nothing of the sort, Tomba," retorted Overton dryly. "You are going to Fort Franklin as a military prisoner."

"This is ingratitude!" snarled the little brown man, looking decidedly crestfallen.

"No; it is not. I owe you nothing for my freedom. Corporal Hyman, you will take charge of the prisoner. See that he does not escape."

"Very good, Sergeant," replied Hyman, motioning to two of the men to place themselves on either side of the prisoner.

"Now, Sergeant Terry, inform me how you came to be here with this detachment?"

"I was sent into town, Sergeant Overton, under orders from Captain Cortland. You were missed from parade, and the captain knew that could not happen with you, unless there was something decidedly wrong. So, at seven this evening, the captain directed me to take this detachment and scour the town for you. If we did not find you by half-past nine I was to report back to the post by messenger, and a larger detachment, under an officer, was to be sent in."

"What time is it now?"

"About nine o'clock."

"We shall be back, then," nodded Hal, "within the time mentioned in your orders. But I shall leave some of the detachment here until Captain Cortland has acted upon the report that I shall make."

At that moment Sergeant Hal, glancing into Cerverra's store, caught sight of the bright, eager eyes of the proprietor.

"Corporal Hyman, arrest that man, also," commanded young Overton sharply, pointing into the shop. "The fellow's name is Cerverra, and he had a part in the plot against me."

With two other soldiers Hyman darted into the shop, from which they soon came out with Cerverra, who protested strongly.

Meanwhile Vicente Tomba had discovered a cause of discomfort.

"Señor Sergente," he complained, "during our struggle in the cellar you knocked my cigarettes from my hand. I beg that you let one of your soldiers take this piece of money into a shop and buy me more cigarettes."

"Shall I do it, Sergeant?" inquired Hyman.

"Tomba," laughed Hal, "after all the trouble that that last cigarette cost you I should think you'd feel like cutting out the habit forever. I know I would drop any habit that had gotten me into such a mess. Had you not wanted to smoke underground I would not have had such a fine chance to upset you. Very likely you would have won, instead of me."

"But I want cigarettes, now," retorted Tomba almost fiercely. "It is ungenerous to deprive me of them."

"Shall I let a man get them for him?" asked Hyman.

"Yes; if he insists," nodded Hal. "What an idiot a man is to allow cigarettes to make such a slave of him that he can't pass an hour without one."

A soldier was accordingly dispatched to the nearest tobacconist on Tomba's errand. While this was taking place Hal hurriedly told his chum and Corporal Hyman what had happened to him, and how he had escaped.

In all this time perhaps two score of curious natives had gathered in the street, though all of them kept at a respectful distance. Sergeant Hal examined these people keenly, though he failed to see any of the eight from whom he had had such difficulty in escaping.

"Captain Cortland told me," Noll broke in at last, "that the former military commander here informed him that he had had about a dozen of his men disappear most unaccountably, and that not one of them had ever been heard from afterward. So, when you failed to return, Hal, the captain declared that he was going to sift this business to the bottom before he stopped."

"I guess, then, that all of our poor comrades in the other regiment who have disappeared in this miserable town of Bantoc have gone, as I did, through visiting Cerverra's store. Now, Noll, I am going to leave you here, with eight of the men, to take possession of Cerverra's store and premises until you receive further orders from the post commander. Hyman and I, and the other four men, will take the prisoners out to Fort Franklin. I would leave you a couple more men, Noll, only I do not forget that it is possible that there may be some attempt made to rescue our prisoners."

"If the natives try that——" broke in Corporal Hyman.

"In the event of an attempted rescue, Corporal, direct your men that they are to shoot the two prisoners at the first sign of an attempt at rescue."

Tomba heard Hyman give the order, and spoke in a low tone to Cerverra. Both rascals thereupon looked disconcerted.

36

"You have your instructions, Sergeant Terry," continued Hal Overton. "March the guard, Corporal Hyman."

As the guard started, Hal fell in beside Corporal Hyman, telling him more of what had happened in the cellar under the Moro curio shop.

"I reckon, Sarge, you've made the biggest discovery of the year in this point of the woods," was Hyman's terse comment. "I reckon, too, the captain will see it that way."

It was cooler by night, though this was due mainly to the absence of the sun. The air was full of sticky moisture, and mosquitoes buzzed about and bit viciously.

"I was born and reared in New Jersey," laughed Hal, striking at the winged pests, "and I have had to stand a lot of guying about the mosquitoes of my state. But Jersey has been libeled. Compared with these Philippine pests the Jersey mosquito is mild enough to be a source of delight."

There was no moon up, but the starlight was bright—and how big and glowing the stars are in the tropics!

Marching at an easy route step over the firm, white road, it did not take the returning detachment more than twenty minutes to cover the distance to Fort Franklin.

"Halt your prisoners here, Corporal, and watch 'em until Captain Cortland gives his orders about them," directed Hal. Then the young sergeant turned down the street leading to officers' quarters, for the administrative office of the post had been closed for hours.

Two minutes later Sergeant Hal Overton was detailing what had happened him to the post commander.

"But wait before you go any further, Sergeant," cried Captain Cortland, interrupting his tale. "I want the other officers to hear the whole of this villainous business."

By the use of the telephone the other five commissioned officers on duty at Fort Franklin were soon summoned.

"Now, begin again, Sergeant Overton," ordered Cortland, when all the officers had gathered in his parlor.

The Army boy retold the entire story, leaving out nothing—not even, the reader may be sure, what Vicente Tomba had said to Hal about Draney's connection with the natives.

"Ray, you're officer of the day," broke in the post commander suddenly. "Go out to Corporal Hyman and see that he turns Tomba and Cerverra over at the guard house. Instruct the sergeant of the guard to make absolutely certain that the prisoners have no chance to escape. Also, Ray, you will send Corporal Hyman and his four men back to Sergeant Terry. Direct the sergeant to keep his whole detachment on the ground to-night, setting a regular guard. Hampton, as you're in charge of the commissary and quartermaster details at this post, the first thing in the morning you will make sure that Sergeant Terry's detachment is supplied with rations enough for breakfast. Early in the morning I shall look further into that plague spot of Cerverra's. Now, Sergeant Overton, continue your story."

When it was finished the officers sat in silence for a few moments.

"Well, gentlemen," inquired Captain Cortland at last, "have you anything to offer?"

"Are you going to arrest the man, Draney?" inquired Captain Freeman, of C Company.

"Frankly," replied Cortland, "that is what is puzzling me. What do you think, Freeman?"

"We cannot doubt Sergeant Overton, and he tells us that Tomba boasted that Draney is in league with the natives in some conspiracy here."

"It is a matter of evidence," replied Captain Cortland musingly. "Not one of you gentlemen would doubt Sergeant Overton's word on any question of fact on which he has knowledge. But his report is based only on what Vicente Tomba told him. Now, at the test, not one of you gentlemen doubts that Tomba would deny it all point blank. I believe that Draney is a scoundrel. I never liked the looks of the man from the first moment, but I can't arrest him on account of my bad opinion of him. Nor would any military or civil court hold him on account of what Sergeant Overton says Tomba told him. That evidence would not satisfy the requirements of any court of trial."

"Sir, is Draney really an American or an Englishman?" inquired Lieutenant Hampton.

"I don't know, Hampton, nor do I believe any one else knows for certain. Englishman or American, it is equally bad either way. If he's an American, then I am sorry to say that there are multitudes of people back in our own country who would welcome only too gladly a chance to attack the government for locking an American up on what they would call a flimsy charge. On the other hand, if Draney is an Englishman, and we arrest him on anything but the most satisfactory evidence, then the British government would be sure to make a noise about the affair. Hang it all, I wish we had just a shade more evidence, and I'd have Draney behind steel curtains in the guard house before daybreak, for his plantation is only eight miles out from here. Personally, I haven't a doubt that Draney is behind all the trouble of which we're hearing rumors."

"What can be Draney's object?" asked Captain Freeman.

"Perhaps he hasn't really a sane object," responded Cortland. "Whatever his motive for standing in with the worst of the Moros, and plotting against the government that we represent, there is sure to be something that he regards as being in line with his own advantage."

"Everything connected with this fellow, Draney, seems to be a puzzle," muttered Lieutenant Hampton.

During this discussion the two youngest officers of all, Lieutenants Prescott and Holmes, sat listening intently, and looking from face to face, though neither ventured any opinions. As "youngsters" it was their place to wait until they were asked to speak.

So notable, in fact, did their silence become that at last Captain Cortland remarked:

"Mr. Prescott, Mr. Holmes, you know that you are not forbidden to speak in the presence of your elders."

"I was listening, sir," replied Lieutenant Prescott, with a smile. "I haven't anything to offer sir, but whatever orders I may receive, I'll follow them all the way across the island of Mindanao and out into the ocean as far as I can swim or float."

"That's my answer, too, sir," supplemented Lieutenant Greg Holmes.

"Spoken like soldiers and officers," said Captain Cortland heartily.

And, indeed, these two young officers were soldiers! Young as they were, they commanded the respect of the men in their companies. B and C Companies could be depended upon to follow Prescott and Holmes wherever these two young West Pointers cared to lead them.

"Gentlemen," announced Captain Cortland at last, "we have the two prisoners in the guard house, and we have a guard over Cerverra's place. We'll take counsel of the night and of sleep. In the morning, at eight o'clock, we'll meet here to deliberate further on this puzzling matter. By the morning our whole duty may be extremely clear to us."

The visiting officers arose, saluted and took their leave.

"That is all for to-night, Sergeant Overton," announced the captain. "But on one point I want to caution you. You have heard the discussion here to-night. Do not repeat it to any of the enlisted men."

"No, sir."

"That is all, Sergeant. One of these days I may have the time to tell you what a fine piece of work you have done for us to-day. Good night, Sergeant."

"Good night, sir."

The Army boy saluted, receiving his superior's acknowledgment. Then Hal stepped outside and made his way down the white roadway of ground shell and went to his own squad room in barracks.

"One point, anyway, is highly satisfactory," mused Sergeant Hal, as he crawled in under the mosquito netting that hung over his cot. "Vicente Tomba, the fellow with a dislike for seeing me alive, is safe behind bars in a guard-house cell!"

But was he?

CHAPTER IX
NEWS COMES OF THE UPRISING

Five officers of the garrison at Fort Franklin had assembled in the post commander's office, at eight o'clock the next morning, and awaited the arrival of Lieutenant Ray, who was still, for a matter of another hour, to be officer of the day.

Nor did Ray keep his brother officers waiting more than a moment. Then his brisk step was heard on the shell road outside, followed by his sudden entrance into the office.

But behind him came two soldiers of the guard, dragging between them an insignificant-looking little Filipino who seemed thoroughly terror stricken.

"How's Tomba this morning, Ray?" inquired Captain Cortland, wheeling about. "And who is this prisoner?"

"This, sir," declared Ray, in a tone that quivered with disgust, "is all that is left to us of Tomba!"

"But this isn't Vicente Tomba at all."

"I know it, sir."

"Explain yourself, Ray."

"Why, Captain, I have just made an inspection of prisoners at the guard house. Huddled in the back of the cell where I personally put Tomba last night crouched this shivery little object, looking as if he expected to be called upon to face a firing squad."

Captain Cortland had leaped to his feet, looking mightily concerned.

"But, Mr. Ray, where is Tomba?"

"I wish with all my heart that I knew, sir," replied the officer of the day, even more disturbed than his superior. "Last night I put Tomba in the cell and turned the key in the lock myself. Then I turned the key over to the sergeant of the guard. When I found Tomba missing, and this worthless object in his place, I made an investigation. The sergeant of the guard declared that the key had not been out of his pocket since I gave it to him."

"Who is sergeant of the guard?"

"Sergeant Jones, C Company, sir."

"And Jones is as honest, capable and energetic a man as we have in C Company," spoke up Captain Freeman, in defense of his sergeant.

"Have there been any visitors at the guard house this morning, Ray?" demanded Captain Cortland. "Especially, any native visitors?"

"Yes, sir; so Sergeant Jones informs me. You know, sir, it has been permitted that native prisoners be allowed to have their friends come and bring them their native food and coffee."

"I know," nodded Captain Cortland. "But that rule, gentlemen, is revoked from this minute. Thanks to that rule Tomba has gotten away from us."

"I hope you don't suspect Sergeant Jones, Cortland," interposed Captain Freeman. "Because, if you do, I'm satisfied that you're doing the sergeant an injustice."

"I don't suspect your sergeant, Freeman. I am more to blame than any one else, for having allowed the old rule of my predecessor here to remain in force. Quite a group of natives came, eh, Ray?"

"Seven or eight of them, sir."

"Exactly," nodded Cortland, "and this wretched little half-price native was one of them. He was brought along on purpose. Probably he was threatened with having his throat cut if he didn't do what he was told by the scoundrels. Then, while some of the natives were passing food and drink through the bars to Tomba and the prisoners, Jones must have had his attention attracted."

"Sergeant Jones remembers that he was called to the guard-house door for an instant," interjected Lieutenant Ray.

"Exactly, Ray, and at the same time a light-fingered native slipped a cunning brown hand into the sergeant's pocket and the key was taken. The cell door was swiftly unlocked, this native stole in, and Vicente Tomba stole out. Friends swiftly slipped Tomba one or two articles of clothing with which to help disguise himself. Then the whole party filed quickly out, and by this time Vicente Tomba is headed for the mountains and going fast."

"But Sergeant Jones found the key in his pocket, sir, when I asked him for it."

"Certainly, Ray. The little brown man who was clever enough to pick the pocket of the sergeant of the guard found it even less trouble to return the key."

"Cerverra didn't get away, anyway," muttered Lieutenant Ray, who had grown suddenly tired and careworn in appearance.

"Undoubtedly that's because Tomba is of more importance to the Moro plotters than Cerverra. Besides, Cerverra owns property here, and he can't well afford to be a fugitive from justice."

"What shall I do with this little wretch of a substitute, sir?" queried the officer of the day.

"Have you questioned this prisoner?"

"Yes, sir, and not a word will he say. He only shakes his head and pretends that he cannot understand a word of English or Spanish."

"Then take him back and lock him in the same cell," instructed the post commander. "Keep him there until he does talk."

"Very good, sir."

Barely had Lieutenant Ray reëntered the guard house when two shots sounded on the road toward Bantoc.

"What's that? Trouble starting?" demanded Captain Freeman, darting to the door and listening.

"It may be only a shooting affray, but we must soon know," replied Captain Cortland.

All of the officers save Ray were now out on the veranda of the building.

Two more shots sounded, close together. Then came a light volley, sounding lighter still.

"It may be that Sergeant Terry is having trouble in town," muttered Captain Cortland, wholly alert in a second. "In any case we must let these Moros see a show of military force. Freeman, detail thirty of your men and let Lieutenant Holmes march them into Bantoc in quick time. Each man to carry fifty rounds of ammunition."

"Very good, sir.

"Lieutenant Holmes, you will go first of all to Cerverra's shop, unless the firing seems to be in another direction. But remember that if trouble breaks loose we will take care of it from here, and that your essential orders are not changed until you receive them from me, or from your company commander."

"Very good, sir," replied young Holmes, saluting.

Freeman and his second lieutenant hurried away to execute the orders without loss of time.

At the sound of the shots many of the men from barracks had run out into the street to see if they could find any explanation of the hostile sounds.

"Second platoon, C Company, fall in!" rang the order, repeated three or four times.

That caught several of the curious ones in the street, calling them to the parade ground.

Acting First Sergeant Hal Overton, B Company, was among those in the street. And he was the first to catch sight of a horse coming up the road at a wavering gallop.

"We'll soon know," the Army boy called to those nearest him. "This looks like a messenger coming."

The man who was astride the horse, and who was attired in white duck blouse and trousers, was bending forward over the neck of the animal.

"Second platoon, fall in!" rang Greg Holmes's command on the parade ground, showing how quickly military orders may be carried out.

"The messenger is bleeding," cried Hal. "I can see the stains on his white clothing. And the horse has been hit, too!"

"Trouble with a big 'T,'" muttered Private Kelly.

Sergeant Hal said no more. He walked quickly down the road as horse and rider drew nearer. The mount was running more feebly now. Fifty feet away from the young sergeant the animal pitched suddenly, staggered, then fell.

For an instant it looked as though the rider would also be stretched in the dust. Then he recovered, leaped painfully away from the horse—and just then Hal Overton reached and caught him.

"Shall I carry you, friend?" demanded the Army boy, for the stranger was a white man, doubtless an American.

At the stranger's belt hung a holster, the flap unbuttoned. He was wild-eyed and breathing hard, but there was no sign of cowardice in the man's sternly set face.

Bloodstains showed over three wounds in the trunk of his body. The right shoulder, also, had been touched.

"I can walk—but give me your arm," gasped the wounded man. "Take me to your commanding officer!"

Hal started, but had not far to go, for Captain Cortland was coming forward on the run.

"Take that man to the porch of barracks," called the captain, whose eye, practised in wounds, saw much. "Don't make him walk far."

Kelly sprang to Hal's aid. Between them they lifted the wounded stranger to a seat on their arms. The man put his arms about their necks, and thus they conveyed him to a broad armchair on the porch.

"My man, there, run for a hospital steward," shouted Captain Cortland. Then the post commander came to the wounded stranger.

Now that he found himself at the end of his journey the stranger appeared to lose rapidly the strength of his voice. He lay back in the chair, his eyes half closed.

"Where do you come from, friend?" asked Captain Cortland.

"The Seaforth Plantation."

"I know where the place is—twelve miles from here, in the interior," answered the captain.

"Right," murmured the wounded one.

"Your name?"

"Edwards. I'm bookkeeper and correspondent for Mr. Seaforth."

"Platoon fours right, march!" sounded from the parade ground.

Edwards heard the command, then the steady whump-whump of the feet of marching men. The wounded man turned in his chair and gazed at the detachment marching away in quick time behind Lieutenant Holmes.

"You act quickly, Captain," murmured Edwards gratefully.

"Those men are marching to Bantoc to keep order in the town," replied Captain Cortland. "Tell me, as quickly as you can, what is wrong at Seaforth's."

"We were attacked just before daylight this morning," Edwards replied weakly.

"In force?" pressed the post commander.

"Just at a guess there must have been two or three hundred of the Malay fiends."

"Any of the defending party killed?"

"Not when I left, Captain. But four of our native Moro laborers were shot dead before they could reach the main house. The main house was being defended by Seaforth when I left."

"How many white men there?"

"Seaforth, his son, his superintendent and a blacksmith."

"They all escaped into the house at the attack?"

"Yes."

"Any natives helping Seaforth in the defense?"

"Yes; eight of the most trusted Moro workmen. But, Captain, you never can tell when you can trust any of these natives."

"I know," murmured Cortland, nodding his head.

At this moment the hospital steward arrived on the run, carrying a case of instruments, bottles and bandages. There was no surgeon-officer at Fort Franklin, the post commander being compelled to rely, at need, on a German physician in Bantoc.

"Get right to work, steward," ordered Captain Cortland. "And I must question this man while you work over him. Edwards, are there any American women at Seaforth's?"

"Three."

"Good heavens!" uttered the captain, paling.

"Mrs. Seaforth, the superintendent's wife, and Miss Daly, the school teacher."

"How did you get away?"

"The Moros didn't appear to be in force on the side toward the stable, and I wriggled through in the dark, traveling flat on my stomach. I reached a horse at the stable, saddled fast, and then galloped away just as the Moros turned loose a volley that covered the noise of the horse's hoofs."

Edwards's voice was becoming much weaker. He paused frequently between words. The hospital steward, standing behind the wounded man, glanced up at Captain Cortland, shaking his head.

"Was the road infested with roving parties of guerillas?" inquired Captain Cortland.

"No, sir," replied the bookkeeper. "I didn't run into any trouble until I reached Bantoc. The natives here must have known that the trouble was coming, for concealed rascals fired on me just as I got alongside the town. They wounded me and my horse."

The other officers, with the exception of the absent Lieutenant Holmes, were now at the porch, listening quietly.

"Freeman, I must keep the rest of your company here," explained Captain Cortland. "And Hampton, your duties here are such that I can't very well spare you from post. So I shall have to send Lieutenant Prescott to Seaforth's. Lieutenant Prescott, assemble the company without an instant's delay."

There was little need to speak of delay. Every soldier left on the post and not engaged in actual duty was as near to the spot as he could be, for all were interested in this latest news.

"Mr. Prescott, don't take the time to march your men to the parade ground. Assemble B Company right here. Pick out the sixty men you want. Sergeant Overton will help you. Take sixty men, two days' rations and a hundred and fifty rounds of cartridges per man. Take blankets, ponchos and shelter tents. Detail your men and be ready to march at the earliest possible moment."

As the call for formation sounded Edwards uttered a fervent:

"Thank heaven!"

The hospital steward forced a draught of medicine down the wounded man's throat.

Quickly the sixty men were detailed, those who had been on sick report lately, or those who for any other reason were unfitted for a long, swift march being rejected.

"Detachment, fall out," ordered Lieutenant Prescott. "Sergeant Overton, see to the equipping of the men for this hike. Don't let any man idle any time away. I'll soon be with you in barracks, for minutes may be invaluable."

Edwards had fallen back once more, lying with his eyes closed. The hospital steward, one hand on the wounded one's pulse, looked at Captain Cortland and shook his head.

"Mr. Edwards," called the captain.

There was no answer.

"Is he dead?" asked the post commander in a low voice.

"No, sir, but he is unconscious and there's only a feeble flutter at the pulse."

As if to prove that he was still conscious, Edwards's lips tried to frame the words:

"Thank heav——"

A sigh, and Edwards's head sank forward on his chest.

"He's gone, sir; there's no pulse," said the hospital steward.

Edwards's brave mission was ended. He had carried the word of danger to Fort Franklin, but he could not live to see the relief or vengeance detail set out.

As soon as it was certain that the bookkeeper had really ceased to breathe, Captain Cortland had the hospital steward summon men, who carried the remains away.

From the portion of the barracks allotted to B Company there came hardly a sound of unusual activity. Yet men were preparing for the "hike," as the long, swift march is called, in record time.

"All ready in this room?" called Sergeant Hal at last.

A chorus of low-toned replies answered him.

"Tumble out, then, lively!"

An instant later the men hastened from other squad rooms. There was no flourish of bugles this time. At a quietly spoken word the sixty men fell in. Non-commissioned officers made a hasty inspection, while Captain Cortland and Lieutenant Prescott glanced up and down the line with keen eyes.

"March your detachment, Lieutenant," directed Captain Cortland, a minute later.

"Twos right, route step, quick time—*march*!" called Lieutenant Prescott.

As one man they swung, and their feet were in motion. At the head of the line marched acting First Sergeant Overton, setting a stiff pace.

For an instant Prescott stood still, eying his men as they swept by. Then he ran to the head of the line, falling in beside the young sergeant.

They were off on the Flag's business!

CHAPTER X

THE INSULT TO THE FLAG

It was a deserted road over which the detachment marched.

When there is fighting in Mindanao, and troops are scurrying along the roads, those inhabitants who are non-combatants keep within their doors—at all events, they remain out of sight. It is as though every native feared to be shot as a possible rebel.

But Uncle Sam's troops have no quarrel with men and women following peaceful occupations. If these brown natives understood our people better they would not scurry to cover when the khaki-clad men are passing on fighting bent.

For three miles, or until Bantoc was left well behind, the quick time continued. Then the young lieutenant decided that it would be necessary to slacken the pace for a while. Soldiers must not only reach their destination as early as possible; they must also be fit for fighting on arrival.

It was not difficult to find the way. An almost straight road led out to the Seaforth plantation. Lieutenant Prescott had a map of the country for use in case he found it necessary.

Twice on the way the men halted, for five minutes each time.

Then, about eight miles out, they came upon outlying scenes of plantation life. There were broad fields, rich with crops, but to-day no laborers were to be seen at work.

Then the main buildings of the Draney plantation were sighted.

About the buildings, too, all was unwontedly quiet. In fact, the main house was closed and had the air of being in a state of siege.

"Humph!" muttered the young lieutenant to the boyish sergeant. "If all we hear about Draney is true, or even the half of it, he has no need to fear the Moros."

Just as the detachment was passing opposite the main building the front door opened, and Draney, bearing a rifle in the hollow of his left arm, hastened out, holding up his right hand.

"Detachment halt!" commanded Prescott in a wearied tone. Then the young commanding officer stepped rapidly toward the planter.

"Well, Mr. Draney, what is it?" Prescott inquired.

"I'm thankful you've come, Prescott."

"Mr. Prescott, if you please," interposed the officer coldly.

"I'm mighty glad you've come. Off yonder we've been hearing firing at intervals ever since daylight."

"How recently have you heard it?" queried Prescott.

"Within ten minutes."

"Thank heaven, then!" muttered the lieutenant. "The Seaforth people are holding out."

"Is it at Seaforth's?" demanded Draney, with assumed eagerness.

"So I imagine. But I must hurry on my way. Take care of yourself, Mr. Draney."

Perhaps that last bit of advice was delivered in a tone of some sarcasm. Draney appeared to feel very uneasy.

"Prescott—Mr. Prescott—aren't you going to leave some of your men here to protect this place?"

"I don't believe it will be necessary," replied the lieutenant, and again, no doubt, there was some hidden irony in his words.

"But the Moros may attack us here at any moment," urged Draney pleadingly.

"I hope they won't attack you, Mr. Draney. But, in any event, I have no orders to leave any of my men here."

"Yet, surely, as an officer commanding troops in the field, you have some discretion in the matter."

"I fear it would be an abuse of my discretion to weaken my detachment by leaving men here."

At that moment four or five shots sounded faintly in the distance.

"You must see my present duty as clearly as I do, Mr. Draney," uttered the young lieutenant quickly. "Good-bye, sir."

"Can't you leave me even six men?"

Prescott did not reply, but called:

"March the detachment, Sergeant."

Hal gave the moving order instantly, the lieutenant cutting off the column obliquely and thus rejoining its head.

"The impudence of that fellow!" growled Lieutenant Prescott, under his breath, but Sergeant Hal heard the words.

Two or three minutes later, when the plantation buildings were out of sight, the young sergeant chanced to look back along the line.

As he did so something in the sky caught his attention.

"Look at that, sir," urged Hal, stepping out of the way of the column and pointing backward.

Lieutenant Prescott uttered an exclamation of anger.

"I wish we had men to spare. I certainly would send some of them back to that confounded Draney!" quivered Prescott.

The object at which both gazed was a blood-red kite, flying high, and apparently sent up not far from the Draney house.

"It must be a signal, sir," suggested Sergeant Hal.

"Of course it is!" stormed the lieutenant. "It's the easiest way in the world of sending the news to the brown fiends swarming around Seaforth's that a military column has passed Draney's place."

"I could take a few men, sir, go back and arrest Draney and bring him to you," suggested Hal quietly.

"What would be the use?" demanded the young officer, a scowl of disgust settling on his face. "In the first place, you wouldn't find Draney in an hour, for probably he has hidden himself. Even if you found him sitting on his back porch he'd be prepared to swear that some native had sent up the kite without his knowledge or permission. Sergeant, a fellow of Draney's type is always hard to catch, and it's bad judgment to try to catch him until you have evidence enough to hang him. So, for the present, I'm certain that we'd better let the scoundrel go. But the flying of that kite means that there's danger of an ambuscade. This is the first time I've commanded in the field and I don't intend to be cut to pieces in ambush."

Raising his voice, Lieutenant Prescott called:

"Detachment, halt!"

As the column of twos came to a stop Lieutenant Prescott announced:

"Men, you can see that red kite flying, back at the plantation. It's a signal to a possible enemy ahead of us. The enemy may try to ambush us. Therefore, from now on, every man will move as quietly as he possibly can. No unnecessary word will be spoken in ranks. You will take pains to keep your equipments from jingling. I am going to march you off the road and send a 'point' ahead. Corporal Cotter!"

"Sir?"

"Take the first four files for a 'point' and march two hundred yards ahead of the detachment. Halt and signal back to us if at any time you hear anything, or have any other reason to believe that you are nearing an ambush. Take the first path to the left, which you will find about a quarter of a mile from here. If I have further orders for you I will send them forward."

"Very good, sir."

"March the 'point,' Corporal."

When the last file of Cotter's men was two hundred yards in advance Lieutenant Prescott nodded to Sergeant Hal to march the main column.

Not a soldier, now, but understood that the command was probably close to the enemy. At all events, fighting within the hour seemed almost certain, for occasional shots still sounded in the country ahead.

No word was now spoken. Cotter found the path, and led his men into it. Prescott knew, from his map, that the path would lead his men to Seaforth's, though by a wide detour from the highway.

Sergeant Hal Overton felt a queer little thrill when he realized that they were now nearing an enemy reported to be much superior in numbers. The thrill was not exactly of fear, though there was some uneasiness in it. Every soldier has felt this sensation when marching into battle. But Hal was curious to know how the feeling affected the other men.

If Lieutenant Prescott felt any of it, there was nothing in his face or manner to betray the fact. He appeared to be "all business," and to have a keen sense of responsibility which, however, did not dismay him in the least. No soldier could gaze at that young officer and feel that the detachment was badly commanded. Such is the West Point training.

Kelly and some of the other soldiers who had seen much active service plodded along like so many laborers going unconcernedly to their work.

Some of the newer enlisted men, who had never before been in real action, betrayed their newness only by the eager light that shone in their eyes. These new men, too, took pains to walk still more softly along the forest path than did any of the old hands at campaigning.

To any but the most hardened old soldier there is something "creepy" in plodding along over a narrow path in a rather dense forest, not knowing at what moment a lurking enemy may pour in a volley that will bowl over half of the command.

Yet every man clutches a rifle and feels at his belt enough ammunition for putting up a good and long fight. There is something exultant in the consciousness that, if attacked, one can render back a good account of himself, and that the American soldier has no cause to be afraid of any troops on earth. It is man's work—and it takes a man to do it!

To the "point," naturally, came the real danger—in the first moment of possible ambush along the path. It would run into trouble first. That is what it is for. If the "point" meets an enemy every man in it may be bowled over by a sudden shower of hostile bullets. But the main column is warned, and the commander can bring up the bulk of his force in battle line armed with the knowledge of where the enemy is. When the "point" marches but two hundred yards in advance of the main body of the command then it can be promptly supported if trouble comes.

Now the distant firing broke out again, and briskly.

"The Moro fiends are trying to rush the planter's house before help can reach him!" muttered Lieutenant Prescott to himself. "We'll spoil some of the joy of those savages when we get close enough to send them a raking volley. I hope they're lined up so that we can give them a flank fire before the scoundrels know that we're on the ground at all."

Two miles covered, then a third was left behind.

Now, a nervous or too eager commander might have hurried his men over the remaining ground, but Prescott, at West Point, had been taught the value of cool, deliberate work.

It was noticeable, however, that now the men marched along with more spirit and swing. Those who may have been secretly nervous were at least certain that soon their suspense would be over. A few minutes, and they would be engaged in something more definite than merely tramping in the direction of danger.

Suddenly Corporal Cotter halted his men, and the same gesture was visible at the head of the column behind.

"Softly," whispered Lieutenant Prescott, but his gesture carried further than did his voice. The main column closed slowly up with the "point."

"I couldn't go further, sir, without running into those fellows yonder," whispered the corporal. "I didn't know that you would want me to do it."

Cotter pointed through the rows of trees to a clearing beyond.

In the center of the clearing stood a little building—plainly the schoolhouse in which the few white children on the plantation and probably many native children of the neighborhood were taught, five days in the week, by some clear-eyed Yankee schoolma'am furnished by Uncle Sam's Government.

Seven Moros were visible at or close to the schoolhouse. All of them were armed. One fellow was hurrying up with a can of oil, which, while the soldiers waited and watched, he sprinkled over the woodwork of the doorway, carrying a trail of the oil inside the building.

"That's a Filipino estimate of the value of education," whispered Lieutenant Prescott savagely to his sergeant.

But then something happened that made Hal Overton boil with indignation.

Just as the fellow had finished scattering the oil and was about to strike a match, one of the other Moros seized the fellow's arm, then pointed up to the flag pole over the front of the building.

All of the brown rascals began to chuckle. Then one of them climbed up. With a keen-edged creese he cut the Flag loose, hurling it down to the ground.

Now began an orgy of derision. First the Moros spat upon the Flag; then, howling gleefully, they commenced to dance upon it. Every now and then one of the brown men bent down to slash at the Flag.

It was hard for some sixty of Uncle Sam's men to stand there, with guns in their hands, and witness such desecration as that. Some of the soldiers began to mutter.

"Silence!" hissed Lieutenant Prescott.

One soldier rested his rifle forward, as though bent on taking a shot, but Sergeant Hal, like a flash, knocked up his arm.

"No man is to fire unless ordered," muttered Overton, and Lieutenant Prescott nodded his approval.

Soon the Flag lay torn and trampled, all but covered in the dust of the roadway before the school. Then one of the Moros again struck a match. In a moment the flames began to crackle and the smoke to ascend.

Then, as if satisfied with their work, the brown rascals set out at a steady trot in the direction of Seaforth's.

"Men," spoke Lieutenant Prescott, in a low voice, "it would have been fine to have poured a volley into those wretches, but it would have told their main body our exact location. We must sink all other feelings until we have reached the plantation and rescued those imperiled there. Corporal Cotter, lead your men to the left, through the woods and around the schoolhouse. On the other side you will find a path that you will follow."

As the detachment started Hal saluted.

"Sir, have I your permission to run out into the clearing, recover the Flag and then rejoin you?"

Lieutenant Prescott shot a keen look at the Army boy, then answered briefly: "Yes, Sergeant."

Hal's task was quickly executed. In the open he encountered no one; when he rejoined the column in the woods he reverently carried a Flag, torn, slashed and dirt-stained.

"One of these days, sir," quivered the Army boy to his officer, "I hope to be able to teach those Moros a lesson with this very Flag!"

CHAPTER XI

IN THE FIRST BRUSH WITH MOROS

At times, while the detachment in the woods covered that last mile the firing ahead cropped up briskly. Then it died down into an occasional, sputtering shot or two. But every discharge of a rifle ahead was now distinctly audible to Uncle Sam's men marching to the relief.

At last the marching men came so close that the young lieutenant whispered to the boyish sergeant:

"I'm going to join the 'point,' Overton. Bring the men on at the same interval, but keep your eyes ahead for signals from me."

"Very good, sir."

Ahead the marching men could now see that the trees were thinning out. Still further ahead they knew that there must lie either plantation fields or the houses themselves.

Many a soldier in the column tightened his grip on his rifle as he thought how soon, now, the raiding Moros would find that they had more fighting on hand than they had bargained for.

The "point" presently halted at the edge of the forest and Lieutenant Prescott signaled back by raising his hand with a downward gesture. Sergeant Overton halted the main detachment.

Over a broad field the soldiers looked, but it was now plain that the besieged planter's house lay on the other side of a belt of timber at the further edge of the field. Then the officer signaled for the main column to be brought up.

"I don't see any of the enemy in sight, men," declared Prescott. "You will deploy into line of skirmishers and then we'll run across the field. Be prepared for the order to lie down in case the enemy develops."

A moment later, and the men, in one straight, thin line, with considerable intervals between them, charged silently across the field.

At the edge of the timber they halted again. Lieutenant Prescott, revolver in hand, moved forward, accompanied only by Corporal Cotter.

After some minutes the pair came back again.

"You'll go forward as skirmishers," said Prescott. "Keep your intervals. Forward!"

No further word was spoken, but the lieutenant, at the right of the line and slightly in advance, moved so stealthily that those nearest him felt that the enemy could not be far off.

Suddenly the stick that the lieutenant carried in place of a sword was held aloft, then the point lowered. The advancing line halted.

"When you move forward again," went the low, almost whispered and repeated order down the line, "crouch low and do not hurry. A hundred yards ahead is a position from which we can rake the rascals with a flanking fire. Forward!"

Very soon the advancing soldiers caught sight of the planter's house between the trees. It stood some seven hundred yards from this nearer edge of the clearing.

Now the soldiers, crouching as they moved, until they appeared to be bent nearly double, came in sight of a trench. It spread away obliquely before them, but everything in the trench was visible to them. At a rough estimate there were some seventy-five brown-skinned Moros crouching in the trench behind a line of hard-packed dirt thrown up before them.

At this moment most of the brown fellows were loafing in the trench. Only occasionally one of them showed himself, raising his gun quickly and firing toward the house. The planter's return fire did not come toward Prescott's command, but well to the right of the soldiers.

"The Moros are up to their same old rascally tricks," whispered Lieutenant Prescott to Sergeant Hal Overton. "They fire heavily, once in a while, and then pepper the house occasionally with single shots. Their idea is to keep those in the house firing until the defenders have used up all their ammunition. When the Moros are satisfied that Seaforth's party have no more cartridges, then those brown pirates plan to rush the house, with little loss to themselves, and run creeses through every defender left alive."

A moment later Prescott's order was repeated down the line of soldiers, now lying prone on the ground:

"Load magazines! Remember to fire low. At the pistol shot begin firing at will, but keep cool and try to make every cartridge tell. Better to shoot slowly than to waste any ammunition."

As noiselessly as they could the prostrate men opened the magazines of their rifles and slipped the cartridges in.

Lieutenant Prescott, revolver in hand, waited until he saw that all had had time to obey the order. Then the stick, now in his left hand, pointed forward, and the various squad leaders whispered:

"At four hundred yards, aim!"

It was a tense moment for the new men.

Bang! Lieutenant Prescott's revolver rang out, the muzzle pointed toward the enemy.

Instantly following it came a sputtering of reports, then a settled, heavy fire. The noise of so many soldiers firing at will was like that made on Fourth of July by a hundred packs of cannon crackers all going off at once.

Yet over all the din rose the yells of the surprised Moros in the trench. It had caught them hard, for most of the soldiers were doing good shooting.

Heedless, now, of the fire from the planter's house, the Moros in the trench rose to flee. Some of them dropped where they stood. Others ran away as fast as their brown legs could carry them, some brandishing their rifles with defiance, a few others throwing down their firearms as they started to bolt.

About a dozen of the rascals tried to return the fire of the soldiers, but fired too high. None of the khaki-clad men were hit.

"Cease firing!" shouted Lieutenant Prescott, but he addressed his order to the bugler who stood beside him. No voice could carry over such a din of firing.

Ta-rar-ta-ra-ta! rang the bugle. As the men obeyed the command to cease firing one would again have been reminded of exploding packs of fire crackers, for the fire died down sputteringly, with here and there another report or two from soldiers who felt that they had a fine bead drawn and ached to "get" another enemy or two.

Fully twenty-five of the Moros had fallen, either in the trench at the first crash of fire, or else while running to cover.

These, however, were not the only enemies at hand, for, from a grove off to the left of the planter's house a heavy fire now crashed out, and bullets began to clip twigs from the trees among which the soldiers lay.

Other bullets whizzed by over the heads of Uncle Sam's men as they lay there. There was a peculiarly spiteful sound to the passage of these bullets. "Whew-ew-ew!" they sang, for most of the Moros were using the .43 Remington, with the brass-jacketed, heavy bullet, this being a favorite arm in the islands among the natives. There are always adventurers at Hong Kong who, for a price, will land any number of Remingtons and any amount of ammunition at lonely spots along the coast of the islands.

Shading his eyes with his left hand Lieutenant Prescott tried to locate this other firing party of Moros. Smokeless powder gives no clue to the hiding places of an enemy, and even if there be any kind of echo it is a confusing guide.

But at last Prescott was sure he had located the second Moro fighting party and he pointed out the place to his men.

"Send them a volley over there, all together," ordered the young officer. "Ready; load! At six hundred and fifty yards, aim. Fire!"

Prescott's face beamed with satisfaction as he held his field glass to his eyes and saw where the bullets threw up the dirt.

"Splendidly done, men!" he cried. "We'll send 'em another. Ready; load. Aim—fire!"

Once more the volley crashed out splendidly. Then the men lay on their hot-barreled rifles.

No more shots came their way just then.

"We've silenced their fire for the time being," chuckled the officer. "I wonder if the enemy are retiring?"

In the silence Uncle Sam's men could hear a frantic cheer rise from the interior of the planter's house.

"Yes; I'll warrant they're glad," cried Prescott, his eyes shining mistily. "But we haven't reached them yet!"

It looked easy. All the detachment had to do was to run across a field and halt before the planter's house.

Yet how could the young commanding officer know that he would not lose half his men by ambushed fire while crossing that open space?

CHAPTER XII
THE BROWN MEN AT BAY——FOR HOW LONG?

If Sergeant Hal, or any other soldier in that detachment of sixty men, had felt any nervousness before the fight started, everyone of them had forgotten it by this time.

So far, not a man had they lost, and none had been even lightly hit. The bravery of soldiers is usually founded on their confidence in their officers. Every man in the detachment now knew that Lieutenant Richard Prescott was an officer who would do all that lay before him to do, yet an officer who would not needlessly sacrifice the life or safety of any man in his command. That discovery by the men goes far to make an officer capable. Let the men once think their commander careless about slaughter, and they will not respond as quickly.

"Men," presently spoke the young officer, as coolly and slowly as though he were explaining a man[oe]uvre in his once favorite game of football, "we have now to reach the house yonder, and there's a likelihood of our being fired upon when we move forward. When I give the order you'll run slowly, at the gait set by Sergeant Overton, who will be ahead of you. If you hear the command to lie down, drop in your tracks. But let no man lie down until he hears the word. We may have to employ half a dozen rushes in reaching the house. Rise! Sergeant Overton to the front. Forward! Charge!"

Steadily and gallantly the little line swept forward. Hal Overton, who knew the pace exactly, went forward at a trot that did not vary by as much as a step to the minute.

In the distance half a dozen rifles popped out singly. Some of the bullets whistled by, others struck the ground near them, ploughing up the dirt.

If any soldier looked for Lieutenant Prescott to order them down, he was in error. Another hundred yards they covered. Then a volley rang out from the men hidden in the grove, and Private Danes dropped, though without a cry.

"Lie down!" shouted Prescott steadily, though he remained with his field glass to his eyes, searching the grove. "Sergeant Overton, see how badly Danes is hurt."

Hal strode over to where the wounded man lay.

"Oh, it ain't nothing, Sarge," growled Private Danes disgustedly. "Just enough to give me a toothache in the hip."

Yet the poor fellow pointed to a bloodstained spot right over the center of the hip bone. Danes's left leg would never again be sound enough to march with his comrades. Perhaps the man realized it, but he was a soldier, and therefore made no fuss.

"You'll have to lie quiet, Danes," returned Sergeant Hal. "We'll get you out of this."

Just then Private Kelly raised his head for a look at the adjacent grove.

As he did so a shot rang out over in the grove and Kelly uttered an exclamation of disgust.

"Hit, Kelly?" queried Sergeant Hal, stepping over to him.

Private Kelly spat out two loose front teeth and some blood.

"Ye see what happened, Sarge," retorted Kelly. "It's a good thing the fellow drew a bead on me profile. But I ain't kicking at getting a dentist's services for nothing. No, that ain't my kick."

"What is wrong, then?" laughed Hal.

"Why, that blamed bullet was hot, and the Moro made me swallow it! It was so hot that it burned all the way down! Got any ice, Sarge?"

A burst came from a dozen distant rifles at once. Bullets tore through the air around Lieutenant Prescott as he stood, still with his field glass to his eyes. Looking around, however, he saw Hal standing, and commanded severely:

"If you're through with your work, Sergeant Overton, lie down. Ready, men, for just one volley. Load; aim—at the front timber line of that grove. Fire!"

Hardly had the crashing volley ripped out when again the young officer's voice was heard:

"Rise, forward, charge!"

This time the line moved with a yell, the two men who carried Danes yelling as loudly as the rest.

"Halt! Lie down!"

They were within two hundred yards of the Seaforth house now. The front door of that building had been thrown open, though no one appeared as yet in the doorway.

It began to look as though the Moros had withdrawn, or else were waiting for something, for no shots came from the enemy.

Again, at command, the detachment rose and rushed forward, this time without cheering.

"Lie down!"

Uncle Sam's men dropped in their tracks, close to the house.

Now, Seaforth, the planter, appeared in the doorway.

"Captain, I hope I needn't tell you that you and your men are welcome," came Seaforth's greeting. He was hardly a middle-aged man, but three years of planter's life in Mindanao had brought deep gray streaks into his hair.

"I've a wounded man to bring inside," announced young Prescott.

"Bring him right in, sir; we'll make him as comfortable as we can."

Private Danes fainted while being lifted and carried into the house. He was soon after revived, however. The two men who had brought him in now used a first-aid package in dressing the wound, after they had washed it.

In the meantime Lieutenant Prescott discovered that none of the whites in the house had been hit, though one of the loyal Moro defenders of the house had been killed and two others wounded.

Then the lieutenant told of Edwards's death. A young woman in the room promptly fainted.

"That's Miss Daly, the school teacher," explained Mr. Seaforth. "She and Edwards were engaged to be married."

Outside more shots sounded. Lieutenant Prescott ran to the door.

Sergeant Hal, however, had detailed twenty of his men to answer the fire, whenever they saw anything to shoot at, while the others had been ordered to get to work with their intrenching tools.

This tool, in appearance, is about half way between a bayonet and a trowel. With it a soldier can lie on the ground, digging and throwing up dirt before him, while he opens a shallow trench in which to lie and conceal himself from the enemy's fire.

"Don't waste any ammunition, Sergeant. Have your men shoot to hit," directed the officer. "I'm going back into the house, but send for me if you see any suspicious move on the part of the Moros."

"Yes, sir," and Sergeant Overton turned his face towards the enemy.

Though he made his men remain prostrate on the ground, Hal Overton stood up. He was using the lieutenant's field glass.

The walls of the planter's house were riddled with bullets, for this house had not been constructed as a fort. Along the outer walls, however, bags of earth had been piled in such a way as to afford comparative safety to the defenders.

"Those of us who weren't fighting," explained Mr. Seaforth, "have been engaged for hours in digging dirt in the cellar and bringing it up in the sacks. But it was a fearful morning until you arrived. Now, our only danger is from a stray bullet. The Moros won't come any closer—they won't dare to charge the house with such a force of troops here to defend the place."

Lieutenant Prescott Climbed One of the Wooden Porch Columns.

"Not unless the rascals are reinforced," replied Prescott. "There is no telling how many of the natives are concerned in this uprising. Hello—pardon me a moment."

Through the open doorway Prescott had caught sight of something moving down the highway. He ran speedily outside, got his glasses from Sergeant Hal and returned to the porch, where he climbed one of the wooden columns. Now he brought the glass to his eyes.

"What do you see?" asked Mr. Seaforth.

"I see," chuckled the lieutenant quietly, "that it was well for us that we left the road and came through the forest. Yonder are at least two hundred Moros marching along. There, they are debouching into the forest and will soon be added to the attacking party here. Those fellows went down the road to ambush us on the way, for they received a signal that we were on the road. We fooled them, but we shall have to reckon with them here, and within fifteen minutes. Mr. Seaforth, send all your people down into the cellar of the house. There they will be safe. This is a job for the Army alone!"

"But——"

"I am in command here, sir, and I direct you to send all of your own people to the cellar at once. That will free our minds of any dread for the safety of your people, and will leave us open to handle the problem that is coming to us."

Then, quite regardless of the fine mark that he presented to possible sharpshooters over in the grove, Lieutenant Prescott stepped outside.

"Sergeant Overton!"

"Sir?"

Hal stepped beside his officer. Thereupon the enemy's riflemen took heart and drove in a score of bullets. Lieutenant Prescott's hat was shot from his head. Two bullets passed through the edge of the sergeant's right trousers' leg, one hole showing just above the other. The back of Hal's left hand was grazed just enough to show the blood. The stick that the lieutenant carried was cut in two by a bullet and half of the stick carried away from him.

"Sergeant," chuckled the lieutenant, "you've heard the expression, 'observed of all observers.' Now you know just how it feels."

"Yes, sir."

"Now, we've got to be quick, Sergeant. We must throw our men all around the house, and dig trenches as fast as we can. Unless I miss my guess, the enemy will—well, what?"

"The Moros will try to overwhelm us with a reckless charge, sir," answered the young sergeant.

CHAPTER XIII

A TALE OF MORO BLACKMAIL

"That's what they will do—if anything," nodded Lieutenant Prescott. "A charge is the wisest thing for the brown rascals, if they are bent on winning here. They know now about how many men I have, and they know that my men are regulars. The Moros have plenty of rifles, and I judge that they're well off in ammunition, but they can't shoot as well as American regulars. On a charge, however—in close, hand-to-hand fighting—these Malays are not to be despised. They always fought hand-to-hand in the old days, and it's in their blood."

With that expression of his views, Prescott, aided by his acting first sergeant, began to hustle the soldiers into line around the house, forming the men in a rectangle at about fifteen yards distant from the walls of the building.

The soldier of to-day must often fight lying on his stomach. These men of B Company crawled to their stations, dragging their rifles after them.

Pop! pop! pop! The Moros were watching, and fired from time to time, irregularly. A prostrate man is hard to hit at a few hundred yards. These pot-shots serve to bother and irritate soldiers getting into position.

As soon as each soldier was in place he began burrowing with his intrenching tool. It is surprising how quickly a man lying down can dig a little ditch and throw up the dirt on the outside.

First, each man dug his own ditch. As soon as he had this completed he connected his ditch with that of the men next to him. Within thirty minutes the men of B Company, without having a man hit by the pot-shots of the enemy, were well intrenched. From time to time some of the soldiers, under orders, ceased their digging to take a few shots themselves, just to keep the Moros from growing too bold.

As soon as the encircling trench had been dug Prescott detailed four men, with picks and shovels furnished by the elder Seaforth, to throw up a trench wall in front of the main door of the house, so as to permit any one safely to enter or leave the house by that door.

"That'll do, Sergeant," nodded Lieutenant Prescott at last.

"It would take a three-inch field piece, sir, to make an impression on this wall of dirt," smiled Sergeant Hal.

"Now, I'll look after this part of the ground, Sergeant; you go around to the south side—and be vigilant."

Hal Overton stepped out from behind the wall, carrying his rifle in the hollow of his left arm. As he showed himself above the low wall of the regular trench, exposing his head and trunk, the Moros began to take notice.

Pop! pop! pop! Bullets struck all about the young sergeant, sprinkling dirt over him.

"Keep your head below the top of the trench wall, Sergeant!" called Lieutenant Prescott sternly. "We can't afford to have you hit. Shield yourself. Don't be afraid of any one suspecting you of cold feet!"

So Hal, though he made a slight grimace, contented himself with crouching low and progressing slowly.

Barely had Sergeant Hal gained his own post, with Private Kelly on his right hand, when a furious fusillade broke out from the southward.

"Keep your heads down, all of you!" shouted the young sergeant. "Don't be too curious about what the Moros are doing. If you keep your heads down the rascals can't hit you, and it won't do us any harm to let them waste their ammunition. Don't any man fire without orders."

"They're doing some good shooting, Sarge, at last," remarked Private Kelly, as the showers of bullets peppered the top of the trench and sprinkled dirt over the crouching soldiers.

"The only good shooting, Kelly, is that which cuts up the enemy," rejoined Hal. "The goo-goos are not hitting any of us, and we're not losing anything by saving our ammunition."

"Goo-goos" is an old name applied to the Philippine raiders. Whenever a native grows tired of fighting, or wants to enter a town for the purpose of getting information, he hides his arms, then enters Uncle Sam's lines, pretending that he is a "good" man, and not a rebel against the authority of the United States Government. From this the soldiers have learned to allude to all fighting Filipinos as goo-goos.

"Lend me your trenching tool, Kelly?"

"Sure, Sarge."

With this implement Hal Overton burrowed a small hole through the top of the trench. Thus, without exposing himself too much, he was able to keep an eye on the distant grove in which the Moros had found cover.

"I'll let you spell me on this watch, from time to time, Kelly," said Hal.

"I'll be glad to, Sarge, for I'll admit that I'm anxious to know what the goo-goos are doing."

"At present they're not trying to advance," replied Sergeant Overton, "and that's about all we're interested in. As long as they stay where they are, and waste their ammunition, they'll not bother us much."

In the meantime Lieutenant Prescott was seated in a chair behind the high wall of dirt before the house door. The elder Seaforth occupied another chair.

"Have you any idea, sir, how you incurred the wrath of these Moro rascals?" asked the young lieutenant.

"By refusing to pay blackmail," replied the planter bluntly.

"Then you were asked to pay money to some of these native chieftains?"

"No."

"Eh?"

"I wasn't asked; I was commanded to do so," replied Mr. Seaforth slowly. "When you speak of the Moro rascals, Lieutenant, don't conclude that all of the Moros are bad, or even troublesome. The truth is that most of the Moros on the island of Mindanao are good fellows. They're lazy, but not notably vicious. There are a few of the old-time chiefs—dattos, they call 'em—who make trouble every now and then. These dattos never respected the Spanish Government, and they don't feel any more kindly towards the United States Government. That is because these dattos have always lived by plunder, and they always intend to do so. For one thing, these raiding dattos don't like to have white men on Mindanao. The spread of civilization here means that the old-time dattos will be driven into the wilds, and that there won't be any more plunder or blackmail money to live on. These Moros out yonder wouldn't have bothered me, this time, if I had paid the money their chief demanded."

"How much did he want, Mr. Seaforth?"

"Ten thousand dollars."

"Whew! That would be a good deal of money to pay out."

"For the sake of peace, and a chance to carry on my plantation business, Lieutenant, I might have paid it—if once would have been enough. But it wouldn't have been. If I had acceded to his demand the datto would have let me alone for this year. He would have sent the same demand next year, however. In fact, the datto would have put me down on his list as being good for ten thousand dollars a year tribute. The first year that I failed to pay this tribute my plantation would be destroyed, and myself, my family and friends put to the knife. So it's either fight or get out of here for good. It seems a strange thing, doesn't it, Lieutenant, to live under the Stars and Stripes, and yet to have to pay tribute to a savage for the right to do business?"

"It isn't right, it can't be, sir—and by the great howitzer, Uncle Sam will put a stop to all this business!" replied Lieutenant Prescott hotly.

"I hope so," returned Mr. Seaforth. "The Datto Hakkut, however, has been doing business here on Mindanao since before the Spaniards left, and my opinion is that he will do business as long as he lives. This fellow Hakkut is a wily old scoundrel, who often falls into traps set for him by our soldiers. Yet, just when the soldiers are about to close the trap, they find that Hakkut isn't there. His escapes are marvelous."

"Did Hakkut himself come to see you, Mr. Seaforth?" inquired the young lieutenant.

"Hakkut? I've never seen the fellow, nor has any other white man around here, so far as I know."

"Then he sends a regular collector for the money?"

"Yes. He has a new collector this year."

"A Moro?"

"The fellow looks to me more like a Tagalo. He's a sharp, keen, little business man—of his peculiar type."

"A Tagalo?" mused Lieutenant Prescott. "By Jove, I wish you'd give me a close description of the fellow."

"Perhaps I can do better than that," proposed Mr. Seaforth, rising. "When the collector was here my son succeeded—without the rascal's knowledge—in getting a snapshot at him. I think I can find the photo."

Disappearing into the house, the planter soon returned, handing the young officer a card. Prescott gazed at the photo, then called out:

"Men, pass the word for Sergeant Overton to report here. Tell him that his orders are to keep under cover while on the way here."

Hal soon appeared, crouching behind the trench, and sheltered by the high dirt wall.

"Sergeant, have you ever seen this fellow in the photo?" inquired the lieutenant, with a smile, passing the card to Overton.

"I should think I have, sir. This is Vicente Tomba."

"Can't be a doubt about it, can there?"

"Not unless Tomba has a twin brother, sir."

"And to think that we had that little rascal in arrest!" muttered the lieutenant. "It was a sad day for Mindanao when Tomba escaped from our guard house."

Then, after a pause, Prescott continued:

"By the way, Mr. Seaforth, how long has Draney been on his present plantation?"

"I don't know, Lieutenant. He's been there longer than I have resided here."

"Has he ever been troubled by the Moros?"

"They have never attacked him, Lieutenant. Draney must pay some tribute to the Datto Hakkut."

Lieutenant Prescott and Sergeant Hal Overton glanced quickly at one another, though neither spoke.

"That is all, Sergeant," said the officer, by way of dismissal. "Return to your men."

"Very good, sir."

CHAPTER XIV

THE CALL FOR MIDNIGHT COURAGE

At a few minutes past six it was dark, for the sun goes down early in the tropics.

Now the soldiers were relieved from their cramped positions of the day. A few at a time they left the trenches, rising and walking about.

Inside the house their bacon was cooked for them and their coffee made. Mr. Seaforth, who was abundantly supplied with food, added a variety of palatable eatables to their night meal.

Lieutenant Prescott and Sergeant Hal Overton walked together around the line of defenses. The officer frequently used his night glass, now and then passing it to the boyish sergeant.

"You see, Overton," said the lieutenant, "from all outward appearances there isn't a Moro left in the woods anywhere around here. Our good judgment tells us, however, now that night has come, that we shall do well to be doubly alert."

"Do you think they will dare attack so large a force in a sudden rush, sir?"

"It is the only trick by which the rascals could hope to beat out an intrenched force of regulars, Overton. By a rush they could have taken the house before we arrived, but I fancy that the first attack was made only as a bluff. They hoped to be able to scare Mr. Seaforth into paying the blackmail their datto had demanded. Now that the troops are here, they realize that their bluff has been met, and that they've got to fight or quit. I believe that the chances are about even on fight or quit. I'd like to hurry up their quitting by a charge, but it might cost us some men, and my orders go only as far as defending the plantation and the white people here. Sergeant, I have about decided to send a report to Captain Cortland. I believe it would be safer to send one or two soldiers, if they're the right kind of men, than to send a detachment. A detachment would be almost certain to be attacked on the way. Two or three bright men might slip away unseen, and get word to the captain and back to me. You know the men better than I do. Whom do you suggest?"

"I'd like to go myself, sir," proposed Sergeant Hal, his eyes blazing with eagerness.

"Absolutely out of the question, Sergeant. You're second in command here, and there's no knowing at what moment I may be hit. Who's a good man, outside of yourself?"

"Private Kelly."

"Send for him."

Kelly lost no time in reporting.

"Private Kelly, do you think you can slip through the enemy's lines and carry a message from me to Captain Cortland?"

"I can, if any man in B Company can, sir," replied the soldier promptly, though without excitement.

"Who is the man you'd like best to have with you?"

"Slosson, sir."

"See if he wants the detail. I prefer that this shall be volunteer work."

In a few minutes Kelly returned, accompanied by Slosson.

"Do you want to go, Slosson?" inquired Lieutenant Prescott.

"Yes, sir," responded the soldier promptly.

"It's an extra-dangerous detail, and you may lose your life."

"I'll chance it, sir. I broke my pipe in one of the rushes here, and I want to get back to barracks and get another."

Lieutenant Prescott could not repress a laugh over such a reason. Slosson joined in, good-humoredly and respectfully.

"Very good; you two men report here in half an hour and I'll have my message ready. Better fill your canteens with coffee before you start. Take nothing else but your cartridge belts, rifles and bayonets."

"Very good, sir," answered both soldiers, saluting and withdrawing.

Punctual to the moment, both men were back again. Lieutenant Prescott had prepared his report, which he handed to Kelly, who fastened it in an inner pocket with a safety pin.

"Now, you'll want to start at once, for it won't be safe to return here later than just before the coming of dawn," said Lieutenant Prescott.

"Yes, sir," answered both men coolly.

"Take care of yourselves, men!"

"Yes, sir."

"We'll watch and listen until you get safely away. If any trouble starts near here hold your ground and rely upon my sending men to your aid."

"Very good, sir."

Lieutenant Prescott and Sergeant Overton watched the two soldiers step over the entrenchment, crouch, and vanish into the darkness.

"I hope they get through," sighed the young officer. "By the way, Sergeant, from the fact of your recommending the men I didn't ask you whether either man is likely to drink any intoxicant at Bontac and unfit himself for the return."

"Neither man touches liquor, sir."

"Then they're to be depended upon. I never trust work of importance to a man who drinks."

"There's a bed in the house for you, whenever you wish it to-night," announced Mr. Seaforth, stepping outside.

"Thank you, sir, but when in the field I sleep with my men. I shall spread my poncho and blanket on the ground presently. Sergeant Overton, I leave you in command until half past one in the morning. At that hour rouse me, report, and then turn in yourself."

"Very good, sir."

"Of course, if anything turns up in the meantime, you'll call me."

"Yes, sir."

For some minutes more the two young Americans stood listening for sounds of possible trouble which Kelly and Slosson might have encountered. Then the lieutenant spread his bed and lay down without removing any of his clothing, placing his revolver beside him on the ground.

Hal set guards on all sides, while the rest of the men turned in, which they were glad to do.

Another army now invaded them! Mosquitoes—myriads of them—buzzed busily about, seeking whom they might devour! The mosquito of the Philippines is well entitled to be called an insect of prey. He is a big fellow, tireless, always hungry and a valiant fighter. The men who lay on the ground carefully wrapped themselves in their blankets, with their hands tucked in. Their heads and necks were protected by collapsible nets that they had taken from their haversacks.

For those who were up and on duty the torment of the flying pests was acute. There was little danger of a sentry going to sleep without a head net and some protection for his hands.

"Ain't it awful, Sarge?" demanded Private Bender, as Hal paused near him.

"That word isn't strong enough," grinned Hal ruefully, as he "swatted" at mosquitoes three times in quick succession.

"I don't mind the Moros," continued Bender, "and I try to be a good soldier, but I'm afraid I'd surrender to the 'skeets' if they had intelligence enough to recognize the white flag."

"We get only two years of this at a time," laughed Sergeant Hal. "Then we can go back to the United States for a vacation."

"I used to think, back in God's country, that a soldier's day and night were full of work," remarked Bender wistfully; "but I'd rather go back there and go to work than have to stand these 'skeets.'"

"They're not so bad in barracks," Hal answered. "It's only in the field that the pests can torment us like this."

"From present signs," commented Private Bender, "I'm thinking that we'll put in a large part of our two years in the field. These Moros are ugly and determined when they get started."

"They're not bothering us much just now," replied Hal, as he started on his round of inspection.

Nine o'clock came and passed. Not a shot had been fired since late in the afternoon. Nor had there been any sound to indicate that Kelly or Slosson had encountered trouble near the plantation. Now that he was in command, Overton did not allow himself to be lulled into indifference by the stillness of the dark night. A sleeping volcano might start into eruption at any moment. At every important point along the trenches Hal paused, using the night glass that the lieutenant had loaned him.

Ten o'clock came and passed without trouble. Then eleven and finally midnight passed. Sergeant Hal, however, was not to be caught napping. He resolved to be vigilant until Lieutenant Prescott relieved him.

Hal had just glanced again at his watch, noting that the hour was nearly one, when a quiet voice reached him:

"Private Bender calls the sergeant!"

Hal Overton ran quickly around to the place where Bender stood peering off into the darkness.

"Use your glass yonder, Sarge," urged the soldier. "See if you see anything moving."

"I do," Hal answered quietly. "I see figures crawling out of the woods, headed this way. Pass the word to rouse every man without noise. Then go to Lieutenant Prescott, with my compliments, and report that the enemy seem to be crawling this way."

Barely had Bender disappeared when Lieutenant Prescott came up on a quick trot.

"Starting things, are they, Sergeant?" the officer whispered.

"Here's your glass; look over there, sir."

Lieutenant Prescott looked quietly for a few seconds. Then he turned to whisper:

"Pass quickly along the lines, Sergeant, and order every man to load his magazine. Instruct the squad leaders not to let their men get rattled and shoot too soon or too fast. This move may be only a ruse."

Bringing his hand smartly to the brim of his campaign hat, Sergeant Overton was off with the orders. He soon returned, however, and took up his position beside the lieutenant.

Then, in a twinkling, scattering Moro volleys sounded on the other side of the house, followed by wild, savage yells.

"That's probably a ruse to draw us around there," muttered Prescott. "Sergeant Dinsmore is there in charge, and he'll know what to do. Good! He's attending to it."

For now the sharper tones of the Army rifles began to rip out on the further side of the house.

Suddenly another volley of shots rang out on the near side of the house, showers of bullets driving in.

"Lie down, Sergeant!" ordered Lieutenant Prescott, falling back.

"Are you hit, sir?" asked Hal anxiously.

"No, no; look after your fire control. Let your men fire whenever they see anything to hit, but not in volleys. Shoot sharp, men!"

Hal's regulars, crouching in the trench, needed no further orders. They could now see, dimly, the figures of the oncoming Moros, advancing by rushes.

The enemy's fire became so heavy that Lieutenant Prescott decided it to be an act of prudence to crouch down himself, though he lay against the trench wall, his head and arms fully exposed as he kept the night glass to his eyes.

"Low aim, men!" warned Hal, as he passed behind the firing line. "Careful with every cartridge. Every brown man you hit is one less to meet with cold steel!"

This is one of the first lessons that the soldier must learn on the firing line. Every cartridge that he fires needlessly means one less shot with which to defend himself. Every man he hits is one less to be reckoned with later.

"Don't fire heavily until the rascals get nearer," was Sergeant Hal's next warning. "Those fellows are not very dangerous until they get close. Then we'll have need of cool gun barrels and plenty of cartridges. Steady!"

"That boy has the making of a commander in him," thought Lieutenant Prescott approvingly. "He's cool and all business. The only thing in the world that he's thinking of is how to make the squad work count. He isn't losing his head."

Night firing is always uncertain. It is too dark to see the end sight on the rifle and advancing figures show uncertainly, like wavering shadows.

"Don't fire so fast," called Hal, as the rifle work of the troops became more brisk. "Fire just enough to annoy the rascals. Save your real work until the enemy are within a hundred and fifty yards."

"Whee! When the goo-goos get that close they'll jump in and scalp us!" muttered a young soldier nervously.

Hal crouched beside the young soldier, resting a hand on his shoulder.

"Don't get nervous, Hunter," urged the young sergeant kindly. "Leave all emotion and quivers for the volunteers and for civilians. The regulars have smaller losses in battle because they depend upon their leaders and do just what they're told. Remember it, lad."

Then Hal was gone, but Hunter found himself flushing a little, yet wonderfully steady in his nerves. He shot carefully, sighting as best he could for every shot.

After another rush, during which they yelled like fiends, the Moros dropped to earth and began firing more heavily.

During that brief rush, however, the Moros lost several men, dropped by Yankee bullets.

"Cease firing and cool your rifles!" shouted Lieutenant Prescott. "Load your magazines, and be ready to drop 'em when they try another rush."

A minute later Datto Hakkut's followers discovered that the American fire had ceased. Yelling, the brown men rose and charged like a cyclone.

"Begin firing! Give it to 'em—*hot*!" shouted the young officer, leading the firing coolly with his revolver.

Again the Moros dropped to earth, though not until they had lost a score of men. For a few moments they lay there, not attempting to keep up much of a fire, for now that they were close to Uncle Sam's regulars, who were firing steadily, it would have been suicide for a brown man to raise his head at all.

"Ta-ra-ta-ra-ta!" The bugler, sticking close to the officer, had to sound the order this time, for the cessation of firing.

"Every man lay his bayonet in front of him, ready to fix!" called Lieutenant Prescott, as the pop-pop-popping began to cease.

That meant cold steel—the final rush in which the regulars must meet several times their own number in deadly hand-to-hand conflict.

CHAPTER XV
IN A CLINCH WITH COLD STEEL

Then came the Moro rush!

All soldiers cheer in the charge, but these brown men had their own kind of battle-cry—a deafening, blood-curdling din.

Yet the regulars made a noise that was heard even over the Moro yelling. There was a smart sound of firing as the magazines of the soldiers' rifles were once more emptied.

The slaughter by men coolly firing at this close range, even in the darkness, was a heavy one. It testified to the courage of these Moros that they could take such punishment and not run.

True, many of the brown-skinned foe did waver, yet through their lines rushed groups of yelling fanatics, armed now only with straight or curved swords and knives. These men of cold steel rushed valiantly into close quarters.

To the soldiers the order to fix bayonets was never given; the men fixed their bayonets by instinct as they emptied their magazines.

Now steel met steel, in a cold, ringing, deadly clash. Occasionally the cry of a stricken man rent the air, though the majority bore their hurts with grunts or in stoical silence.

The greater part of the regulars leaped to the top of the trench wall to meet the shock. That move, however, soon carried them beyond the entrenchments.

Some of the regulars found themselves fighting three or more of the enemy at once. Lieutenant Prescott shot one Moro dead, but as he did so Sergeant Hal saw another Moro, armed with a sword, rush at the lieutenant from behind.

Overton leaped forward, cracking the fellow's head with the butt of his clubbed gun. Just as he did so Prescott fired squarely over Hal's left shoulder, knocking over a Moro bent on stabbing the sergeant from behind. The noise of that explosion, so close to his ear, deafened the young sergeant temporarily.

Both officer and sergeant realized that each in turn had saved the other's life, but there was no time for acknowledgments. The foe had yet to be met and worsted in that furious conflict.

At last it was over. The Moro men had broken and fled, their yells dying out in the distance.

Fully two dozen of the soldiers started to pursue. Prescott turned, bawling an order to the bugler over the din. The notes of the bugle recalled the soldiers.

"Men," shouted Lieutenant Prescott, "the first duty is to get the wounded behind the trench and then into the house. Every man badly hurt must have prompt attention."

Then, indeed, came the time to take account of what had happened.

Three of the soldiers already lay dead, their heads and bodies frightfully gashed. Another, Bender, was dying from two knife thrusts through his lungs.

Four more men were too badly hurt to help themselves. A dozen others had wounds of varying degrees of seriousness but were able to reach shelter unaided.

Uncle Sam had won the victory for the moment, but he had paid dearly for it.

"I'm glad you gave me that word when you did, Sergeant," murmured Private Hunter. "It steadied me. If it hadn't been for that I guess I'd have been a goner by this time."

It was after three o'clock in the morning when Sergeant Overton felt that he finally had a moment for free breathing.

"Sergeant," said the lieutenant, "your watch tour is long past. Lie down and get some sleep."

"You're sure that I can be spared, sir?"

"Certainly; you can be called if you're needed."

To one not accustomed to war it might seem strange, but thirty seconds after Hal had wrapped himself in his blanket he was deep in dreamless slumber. He slept until the sun was fairly high. Then Prescott awoke him.

"Kelly—Slosson—are they back, sir?" were Hal's first words, as he threw aside his blanket.

"Back nearly three hours ago, Sergeant," smiled the officer. "It's half-past eight. I've been occupied, and have missed my breakfast. Come into the house and breakfast with me, Sergeant Overton. Sergeant Dinsmore will look after things outdoors."

"Did—have you buried the Moros who fell?" questioned Hal, looking out beyond the trench.

"The rascals sent over men with two lanterns, and asked permission to carry off their casualties," explained the officer. "I let them do it."

"It must have given them a lot of work to do," muttered Hal.

"It did. I estimate their dead at thirty, and their badly hurt at forty or more. We made it an expensive night for them."

"We paid a big price on our own part, sir," returned the young sergeant, "for we paid in good Americans."

"We can't have war without death, can we?" half sighed the West Pointer.

Once inside the house Hal's first care was to visit the wounded men.

"Bender's gone, sir?" asked Hal.

"Yes," nodded Lieutenant Prescott gravely.

Then they went to breakfast, for the soldier must eat or presently stop fighting.

"You'll want to know my orders from Captain Cortland," said Lieutenant Prescott, filling his cup with coffee.

"Yes, sir; if you feel at liberty to tell me."

"The captain's instructions are few. He tells me that, as commander in the field, I will have to use my own judgment to a great degree. But the captain urges me, as soon as I may be satisfied that the Moros have withdrawn, to leave Sergeant Dinsmore here with a guard of twelve men, and to bring the white people from this plantation into town with me. Then Dinsmore, if he sees no more of the Moros within three days, is to march his men back to Bantoc. With the limited number of men at his disposal Captain Cortland recognizes the impossibility of keeping a military guard regularly at each plantation."

"But, sir, if Dinsmore and a dozen men had to brave such a charge as we met last night he would stand a very good chance of having his detachment wiped out, wouldn't he?"

"No; for the Moros would attempt such a charge only in the night time. Captain Cortland has sent me a supply of various-colored rockets, and a code by which they are to be used. So, if attacked by a rush at night, Sergeant Dinsmore will withdraw with his men to the house, and send up rockets that will be seen in Bantoc and at Fort Franklin. Then a column will be sent out to overtake and punish any brown rascals who may attack."

"Have you seen any signs of the Moros lately, sir?"

"No, Sergeant. Later in the forenoon, however, I think I shall order you to take about twenty men out in skirmish line. You will try to draw the enemy's fire, returning if you succeed. If you do not succeed, you will search the woods, always keeping an alert eye open for the possibility of running into an ambushed party of cold steel men in the woods."

"I shall be delighted to have charge of that reconnaissance, sir," Hal replied promptly.

"Yes; it is work cut out for just such a cool head as yours, Sergeant."

"Thank you, sir."

"Well, you are cool-headed, so why should I not say it?" laughed Lieutenant Prescott. "Sergeant, your presence here has made my own work half as heavy as it would have been without you. I shall so report to Captain Cortland on my return."

"Thank you, sir. May I ask if Captain Cortland reports trouble with the Moros in any other locality?"

"Nothing has as yet broken out anywhere else. Captain Cortland writes me that Bantoc, while apparently quiet, is really a seething volcano, ready to break out into insurrection, riot and pillage. Lieutenant Holmes is still in personal command over in Bantoc, so I fancy your friend, Sergeant Terry, is there with him."

As Hal followed the lieutenant out after breakfast, the first man they saw was Slosson, busily smoking the pipe that he had tramped twenty-four miles to obtain.

Then, as the officer walked away, Kelly sauntered up.

"Did you two have any trouble on the way in or back, Kelly?" asked Sergeant Overton.

"Not the least bit, though we stepped pretty close to some of the 'goo-goos' in getting away from here, Sarge. But we got by without telling 'em we were there."

"You two must be tired."

"We've had the bit of a nap," replied Kelly.

An hour later Lieutenant Prescott again approached Sergeant Hal.

"Count off your twenty men, Sergeant. Line 'em up for instruction. I'm going to send you over yonder, now, to make that scouting reconnaissance. Don't fall into any traps, Sergeant."

Hal quickly detailed his men, ordering them to fall in.

"Why am I not picked, Sarge?" whispered Kelly.

"Man, you've done enough."

Lieutenant Prescott's instructions were few, though to the point.

Then, in line of skirmishers, Sergeant Hal Overton ordered his men forward. Over the trench they went, then advanced steadily toward the woods from which had come the rush of the night before.

Those left behind watched anxiously. Would the issue mean another savage fight—or what?

CHAPTER XVI

DATTO HAKKUT MAKES A NEW MOVE

To the civilian mind, being sent forward purposely to draw the enemy's fire, looks like "ticklish" business.

Yet it is better to risk a few men rather than sacrifice many. It is on the same principle that a "point" of several men is always sent in advance of the larger body when moving supposedly in the face of the enemy. The "point" often draws disastrous fire upon itself, but the larger body of troops is saved from catastrophe.

The soldier accepts calmly this work of going out ahead to draw a possible enemy's fire. It's "all in the game," as he understands it.

Of course, when troops are sent out only for the purpose of drawing fire, these troops withdraw, if necessary, as soon as they attract the enemy's fire to themselves, and thus locate the enemy.

Sergeant Hal Overton kept at the right of his thin, sparse line of men as they moved forward.

Every man had his eyes ahead; each was watching for the first sign of trouble.

"When the line had reached a plane within a hundred yards of the edge of the woods the soldiers expected, momentarily, to hear the signal shot, then the first scattering shots, followed by the heavy, crashing volleys.

Yet they passed this point safely and went on. The edge of the woods was gained, still without provoking hostile shots. It would have looked to one untrained in the art of war as though there were no enemy there. But this handful of soldiers knew better than to jump at any such conclusion. The Moros, like the Tagalos and Pampangos, are fond of getting an enemy at close quarters, and then leaping on him with cold steel. The Tagalo or Pampango fights with the bolo, the Moro often with the creese, and with all these brown-skinned men the game is the same—to leap up unexpectedly, from the tall grass, before the soldier has had time to throw himself on his guard.

A swift, short-armed cutting movement—a mere slash, delivered with muscular effort, and the soldier is gashed across the abdomen. After this cutting has been effectively delivered the white fighting man usually sinks down in a pool of his own blood, and his fighting days are likely to be over.

Small wonder that Uncle Sam's infantrymen prefer facing native bullets to native steel! The bolo man, or the sword man, is the soldier's greatest aversion. It is like fighting rattlesnakes!

Glancing down the line, Sergeant Hal saw one or two of the newer men flinch slightly.

"Steady, there!" Hal called, in an easy but business-like tone. "If we strike the rascals an unbroken line is the one hope for us all."

They had now reached the woods, but no halt was made. The boyish sergeant, who knew his business, marched his little command about six hundred yards under the trees.

Still no Moros were encountered.

Then Hal turned his line to the left, marching on through the woods. In this manner, in less than an hour, he had thoroughly explored the territory near the Seaforth plantation, and had returned to the point where his command had first entered the forest.

"Halt!" ordered the young sergeant. "Fall out, but don't scatter."

Then Overton stepped to the edge of the woods, waving his hat. In the distance Lieutenant Prescott, with his own hat, returned the signal. Then Hal, using one arm in place of a signal flag, wig-wagged the information:

"We have thoroughly scouted all about your position, and find no sign of an enemy."

From the lieutenant came the answer, wig-wagged by arm:

"Good! March your men in."

"I have allowed men to fall out and rest," Hal answered. "They are tired after their hike."

"Rest your men five minutes, then march them in," replied Lieutenant Prescott.

"Very good, sir," Hal signaled.

Exactly five minutes later, Overton commanded:

"Fall in! By twos right, march!"

Within the hour several of the former Moro laborers on the plantation returned. They reported that the Datto Hakkut and some three hundred men were on the march, miles away and evidently headed for the mountains.

"These men are honest and loyal, Lieutenant," explained Mr. Seaforth. "They are my regular laborers. Of course, when the attack came those who could not reach the house took to their heels. But these natives, like many Moros, are dependable. They are not to be classed with the idle, vicious cut-throats that follow the datto."

"Hm!" replied Lieutenant Prescott, politely, but he scanned all of these returned natives, keenly. None of them, however, showed any wounds, or bore any other signs of having seen recent military service with the datto.

"Mr. Seaforth," said the young officer, presently, "I am going to follow the course laid down by Captain Cortland, and return to Bantoc with the greater part of my command. I shall, however, leave Sergeant Dinsmore and a dozen men here. I urge that all the white people of the plantation return with me to town."

"You can take the women with you, Lieutenant, if you will," replied the planter, "but we men feel that we should stay here and make every effort to go on running the plantation."

"If you do not think it too dangerous, Mr. Seaforth."

"No; I can trust my laborers, and they tell me that Hakkut and his rascals appear really bent on reaching the mountains."

"But if they go to the mountains, you know, they go only that they may be more secure until they have recruited other brown rebels. If Hakkut can get enough men together, he will attempt to carry fire and bloodshed even into Bantoc."

"Let the women go with you, and we men will stay here," was the planter's decision.

Half an hour later the column, minus Sergeant Dinsmore and his squad, swung off on the return march. A wagon had been provided for conveying the dead soldiers, another for the wounded, and a third vehicle for the women.

Four hours later the column was at barracks, from which the women were escorted into Bantoc, where there was a military guard, and where they could stop with friends.

Just before dark an escort of twenty men, guarding two wagons, marched into Bantoc. Sergeant Hal had asked and secured permission to head the escort, for he wanted to see his chum, Sergeant Noll Terry.

"Well, so you've been doing some real fighting," demanded Noll in a tone of friendly envy.

"Yes," assented Hal.

"The Moros are not such very classy fighters, are they?"

"They're good enough for me," Hal Overton answered. "I don't mind their rifle fire, but I can do very well with the least possible number of brushes against their cold steel."

"But our fellows have their bayonets."

"Yes; but wait until you have to face a rush against those murderous creeses. I can't tell you much about it. It sounds tame in the telling, Noll, but you'll know all about it when you have to go up against it. How have things been here in Bantoc?"

"Bad," Noll replied, with a shake of his head.

"Any serious trouble?"

"No; no fighting. For that matter, I think most of the Moros here in Bantoc like us well enough, and are disposed to be orderly," replied Terry thoughtfully. "Of course they're the more peaceable part of the population, anyway. On the other hand, there are plenty of Moros here in Bantoc who don't hesitate to let us see how sullen and restless they are. Only a spark is needed, or maybe only a secret word from the datto, and two or three hundred ugly fellows here in Bantoc will try to get the upper hand, or else take to the brush with Hakkut."

"We're going to have a warm time here before we're through, I think," replied Sergeant Hal, with a shake of his head.

"What puzzles me," muttered Noll, "is why the government doesn't send troops enough here to wind up the thing in short order. The whole of our first battalion of the Thirty-fourth, for instance, ought to take the field at once, backed by a platoon of light artillery. We ought to be sent to chase Hakkut clean across the island and into the ocean on the other side of Mindanao."

"It's not for me to criticize the government, or to say what it ought to do," Hal rejoined.

"Yet I can understand, lads, that you're puzzled," broke in the quiet voice of Lieutenant Holmes behind them. "You wonder, both of you, why the government doesn't use more force. Have you any idea of the great number of troops we already have here in the islands? As it is, it takes an Army corps to keep the natives in anything resembling order. Yet, of course, the government, in this especial case, could exert itself and send an expedition of a regiment of infantry, a squadron of cavalry and two batteries of light artillery, say, against Datto Hakkut."

"That would be enough to wind these rebels up in short order, sir," murmured Hal.

"No; it would do nothing of the sort," smiled Lieutenant Holmes. "Hakkut and his crew would laugh at us. What would happen? The rebels would disperse, and soon show up at their homes, all through this island. As for Hakkut, he would go into hiding. He always is in hiding when he isn't in the field defying us. I don't know whether you sergeants know it, but it's a fact that no American Army officer has ever seen Hakkut. He never shows himself, and his hiding place is a good one, for no American knows where it is. So our big expedition that might go out against Hakkut would find none of these rebels to fight. After the troops of the big expedition had been withdrawn, however, then Hakkut and his land pirates would come out again at their own convenience."

"Wouldn't it break up Hakkut's game altogether, sir, if the government kept enough troops here to be able to send a crushing force against him whenever he raised his hand?"

"Possibly it might," nodded Lieutenant Holmes; "but to police all of the Philippine Islands in that fashion we'd have to make the United States Army three times as large as it is to-day—and then station the whole Army in these islands. On the other hand, our present plan of keeping small forces at different points, and sending out small expeditions at need, shows the natives that we don't take them very seriously. We also show them that a hundred of Uncle Sam's regulars is a pretty large force for them to attempt to fight. By attacking the Moros with small expeditions we keep alive and always before them the fact that we know one of our regulars to be equal to several of their pirates."

Both sergeants saluted as Holmes moved on.

"Maybe the lieutenant is right," muttered Noll thoughtfully. "But the present way of fighting these wretches is pretty expensive in the matter of soldiers' lives."

CHAPTER XVII

"LONG" GREEN AND KELLY HAVE INNINGS

"Ugh! That's a beastly trick. No white man would ever do a thing like that!"

The speaker was Private William Green, also known as "Long" Green, from his former habit of carrying large sums of ready cash about him.

Our readers will remember William. He was a good soldier, but above all he was a good Army business man, for he saved his money and added to it. To William Green the men of B Company always went when they were "short" and craved spending money. To any man in B Company "Long" Green would lend five dollars, but he always exacted six in return on pay day.

"What's wrong with your nerves, Green?" inquired Sergeant Hal, stepping out on to the porch of the barracks.

"Slosson has been telling me about kantab," replied Green, with a grimace and a shudder.

"Never heard of him," replied Hal.

"It isn't a 'him' at all, Sarge," rejoined Green. "Kantab is the name of a poison that the Moros extract from one of their plants up in the hills."

"Well, cheer up," urged Sergeant Overton, seating himself and opening a book. "There are no poisons issued in the rations."

"But Slosson was telling me about two soldiers who got kantab in their rations a few years ago," insisted Green.

"Was the quartermaster court-martialed?" asked Sergeant Overton. "Or was it the fault of the company cook?"

"Nothing like it," replied Green. "Two soldiers were on outpost one morning, and they had just prepared their breakfast. Just then they thought they heard a sound in the bushes, so they caught up their rifles and went out to investigate. They found nothing, so they came back to their breakfasts. They thought their coffee tasted rather bitter, but they drank it just the same. Ten minutes later both men were dying in agony. That noise had been a ruse to draw them off, while some native slipped in and put the kantab in their coffee. Ugh! That's a cowardly way to fight. If I find anything bitter about my food, even here in barracks, I'm going to toss the grub out. No kantab for mine," wound up "Long" Green earnestly.

"Did that really happen, Slosson?" asked Sergeant Hal, glancing up from his book.

"Sure," responded Private Slosson nonchalantly.

"I've heard about the stuff, too," nodded Private Kelly. "Only yesterday I heard one native talking about it to another."

"I'm going to watch my chow (food) after this," insisted Green.

For twenty minutes Hal read on, paying no attention to the chatter of soldiers about him. Then a bugle blew, and Hal closed his book with a snap.

"That's sick call, Kelly, and I believe you're on sick report," announced the boyish sergeant.

"I'm not going," returned Kelly. "What's the use. The hospital steward, I've been finding out, has no medicines whatever but salts and quinine. I can't stand the taste of either."

"But you're going to sick call, just the same," Hal retorted dryly. "Your name is on sick report, so to hospital you go. There's no way out of it."

Sick call is sounded morning and afternoon. It is the first sergeant's duty to enter on sick report the names of all enlisted men who report to him that they are not well, or think they are not well. Then, when sick call sounds, the first sergeant marches to hospital with the men whose names he has entered on sick report.

"Fall in, Kelly," ordered the young sergeant.

"I'll not take salts or quinine," insisted Kelly.

"You'll march to sick call, just the same. Fall in!"

So in step, and briskly, Hal and Private Kelly marched over to the little building which, at Fort Benjamin Franklin, was dignified with the name of hospital. The acting hospital steward was there waiting for them.

As this small command did not have a commissioned medical officer the steward attended to all cases of minor illness. When occasion warranted it the German physician was summoned from Bantoc to prescribe for the men.

"The sick list, steward," reported Hal, handing over the official paper on which Kelly's name alone appeared.

"What ails you, Kelly?" asked the steward.

"Nothing," Kelly answered defiantly.

"Then you'll have to discover an ailment soon," frowned the steward, "or I'll ask Sergeant Overton to report you for shamming sick report."

"Why, truth to tell, I didn't feel very well," asserted Kelly. "But that was two hours ago. I'm feeling fine now."

"Let me see your tongue," ordered the steward. He also "took" Kelly's pulse and noted his respirations, entering all this information on his record.

"Any pain anywhere, Kelly?"

"Sorra the bit," promptly rejoined the soldier.

"You're just a little off-key," went on the hospital steward, with a professional air. "Not much; still, you'd better have some medicine."

"I can't take salts," protested Kelly. "They make me sea-sick. Give me salts, and ye'll have to find a bed for me here, and take care of me for a few days."

"Quinine is about your size," replied the steward, reaching for a five-pound can of the stuff.

"That'll kill me, entirely!"

"Four ten-grain doses never killed any man," insisted the steward.

"I won't take it!"

"Oh, yes, you will, Kelly. This is the Army, and discipline is the rule. I'll make sure of the first dose by seeing you take it here."

The hospital steward's tone was firm, and under the regulations he was master of the situation.

"Then, for the love of Mike," gasped Kelly, "give me the bitter stuff in a capsule."

"Certainly, if you like it that way, Kelly," assented the steward, picking up a gelatine ten-grain capsule and packing it tight with the white, bitter powder.

"I don't like it any way," growled Kelly.

"Now, that's nonsense, man. Why, all the medical authorities are agreed that quinine is the greatest blessing to man ever discovered."

"Then why don't the doctors take more of it themselves?" scowled Private Kelly.

"Here you are," continued the steward, capping the capsule and passing it to the unwilling victim.

Kelly dropped the capsule into his mouth, resolving to hold it there until he could get outside.

"Here's a glass of water. Wash it down," ordered the hospital steward. "Then you can open your mouth and I'll make sure that you've swallowed the stuff."

"Can't ye be after taking a soldier's word?" demanded Kelly, with a burst of virtuous indignation.

"Not where quinine's the medicine," returned the steward, grinning. "Now, down with the water, and then open your mouth."

There was no chance for sleight of hand here. Kelly actually swallowed the hated stuff, then submitted the proof.

"Here are the other capsules," went on the steward, handing the victim a small pill box. "Take one of the capsules at bed time and the other two to-morrow morning and noon. Sergeant Overton, it will be as well for you to see that Kelly obeys the order."

"May I go now?" demanded Kelly.

"Yes."

So sergeant and private passed out together.

"No wonder men sometimes desert," grumbled Private Kelly.

"Nonsense," laughed Hal. "Kelly, you're too good a soldier to be afraid of just a bad taste in the mouth."

"I don't want a bitter taste in me mouth, unless an enemy is smart enough to give it to me," grumbled Kelly, then added, "but by the powers, that steward is an enemy of mine, and I'll have his scalp one of these nights when I catch him outside on pass."

When Hal returned to the porch he picked up his book and disappeared into the quieter squad room, for he had found it rather difficult to study while among the others.

"Long" Green was making considerable noise, lying on his back on the porch, rumbling snores issuing from his wide-open mouth.

"No man has a right to run a Gatling gun like that without a license," muttered Kelly, gazing thoughtfully down at the noisy sleeper. "Boys, whist!"

There was mischief in the Irishman's eyes. Sergeant Hal, from the shadow at the back of the squad room, heard and glanced out.

At a sign from Private Kelly, the other soldiers rose, fleeing softly inside of barracks.

With an air as grave as that of a college professor absorbed in a chemical experiment, Private Kelly drew the pill box from one of his pockets. He took out a capsule, uncapped it, and bent over the sleeper.

Into "Long" Green's open mouth Kelly carefully but swiftly emptied the contents of the capsule of quinine, then joined his comrades in the barracks, all but closing the door.

After a moment Private William Green, asleep though he was, became dimly conscious that something was wrong with his tongue.

Then he awoke. There was a hideously bitter taste in his mouth.

In another instant Private Green had turned ghastly pale, shaking like a leaf. It took him but a moment to realize that he was alone on the porch. Out on the road, some two hundred yards away, a solitary male native was passing. Private Green was a quick guesser.

"*Kantab!*" he gasped hoarsely.

Then "Long" Green's legs got into swift action. Vaulting the porch rail, and almost falling in his trembling weakness, William made a straight line for the hospital, vanishing inside.

Five minutes later Hospital Steward Hicks appeared on the scene. He was supporting "Long" by one arm, for the soldier was not yet over his fright.

"Kelly," said Steward Hicks, "I find that I made a mistake. The medical authorities do not prescribe the stuff I gave you in a case like yours. So I'll take the capsules back."

"You're welcome," grinned Kelly, passing over the pill box.

"Two capsules; there should be three," remarked the hospital man, after having raised the lid from the box. "Green, you idiot, the kantab you're howling about came from the missing capsule that Kelly can't return to me."

"Do you give kantab at the hospital, too?" gasped "Long," looking more scared than ever.

"We do," said the steward grimly. "But we medical men call it quinine."

First "Long" looked bewildered. Then as the grinning soldiers gave vent to howls of glee a great light began to dawn on the mind of Private Green.

"Kelly, you scoundrel!" he yelled, leaping\ forward. "I'll take it all back—out of you. On your feet, man!"

But Kelly, convulsed with laughter, sat back in his chair until the irate Green slapped his face. At that the Irishman's resentment leaped to the surface and Kelly followed his recent victim to the ground beyond the porch.

Kelly, however, was weak with inward laughter. Green, therefore, administered some rather severe punishment, and, in the end, sent Kelly to the ground. "Long" couldn't possibly have done this under any other circumstances.

Private Kelly sat there for two or three minutes. Then he got up slowly, his face grave as he stepped to "Long," holding out his hand.

"'Long,' I know now what ailed me," confessed Private Kelly. "'Twas me liver. Your tr-reatment has fixed it up fine. I'll call on ye for another treatment when me liver needs it. By me present feelings I'm thinking 'twill be about to-morrow morning, after guard-mount."

CHAPTER XVIII
SENTRY MIGGS MAKES A GRUESOME FIND

It is not necessary for even the most ardent admirer of Private William Green to feel sorry for the fate of that soldier the next morning after guard-mount at the capable hands of Private Kelly.

Kelly had something else to think about, and so had every other man in the little garrison.

Just before daylight the sentry on number three post had made a horrible discovery. Now that the old guard was relieved, and the new guard was on, the sentry who had made the discovery was able to tell what he knew of it, with such other particulars as had been learned since.

Private Miggs was the sentry in question. Before daylight Miggs had patrolled down to the further end of his post. On his return along post he had discovered something on the ground ahead of him.

When Miggs learned the nature of his discovery he was almost overcome. Being a soldier, he did not faint, but for a few moments he did feel a sensation of nausea.

Then, raising his voice, the sentry called the corporal of the guard to post number three. The corporal and the two members of the guard felt a similar nausea when they arrived on the scene, and it ended in sending for the officer of the day, Lieutenant Dick Prescott.

Without venturing to order the removal of the find, Lieutenant Prescott sent a member of the guard to awaken Captain Cortland.

After the post commander had seen it, the guard removed the ghastly find to the guard house, where it still remained.

What had upset Private Miggs's mental balance was the sight of two severed heads lying on the ground in his path along post. They were the heads of white men.

To each had been tied a piece of coarse paper, and on each paper was rudely traced the likeness of a crab. This crab, as Captain Cortland already knew, was the sign manual of that arch scoundrel of brown skin, the Datto Hakkut. The crab was meant to signify that, while the datto could move forward, he could also crawl sideways or backward—that he was strategist enough to crawl out of any trap that the soldiers might set for him.

As soon as the light came Captain Cortland despatched an armed guard party to bring over to the fort the German physician and three other white residents of Bantoc, to see whether they could identify the severed heads.

The heads proved to be those of two young American doctors of philosophy, Hertford and Sanderson, who had come to Mindanao months before, one for the purpose of securing specimens representing the geological formation of the island, and the other in pursuit of specimens of the plants and flowers.

Despite strong advice to the contrary, as given by the former military commandant at Bantoc, Drs. Hertford and Sanderson, attended only by a small party of natives, had gone into the mountains to gather their specimens. Since then nothing had been heard of the two enthusiastic young scientists—until Sentry Miggs had stumbled upon his gruesome find.

The soldiers discussed little else that morning.

"Of course it was the old brown rascal, Hakkut, who had the young scientific gentlemen killed. Didn't Hakkut have his card tied to each head?" demanded Private Kelly, who was the centre of a group of enlisted men.

The group of officers over in Captain Cortland's office had come to the same conclusion.

"It is the old brown scoundrel's way of showing us his defiance," declared Captain Cortland in a shocked voice. "Why couldn't that pair of enthusiastic boys take good advice and keep out of the mountains? Would their collections of stones and plants be worth as much to any college as the young men's lives would have been worth to themselves?"

"The question is, Cortland, what are we going to do in answer to this defiance?" suggested Captain Freeman, of C Company.

"What are we going to do?" asked Cortland, his face becoming even graver. "We have a very small command here, but there's only one thing we can do. Hakkut has defied us, and, unless he is punished for it, the native respect for American authority in these islands will soon be less than nothing. What are we going to do? There is nothing that we can do but send the strongest column of men that we can spare up into the mountains on the double-quick. We've got to root out that brown scoundrel, and send him and his band running as fast as they can go, or else we shall be forced to admit to the natives that the claim of the American nation to govern Mindanao is only a stupid joke. Our expedition must start before noon!"

"Who will command the column?" inquired Captain Freeman.

"You will command, Freeman. I would give half a year's pay to head the expedition myself, but I am post commander here, and after the greater part of the troops have started the problem here at Bantoc is going to be such a serious one that I feel obliged to remain here and handle it myself."

After thinking a few moments longer, Captain Cortland continued:

"Freeman, you will take sixty men from B Company, and the same number from C Company. I can spare you but two officers, for I shall need the services of Bay and Hampton here. So Holmes will command the C Company detachment, and Prescott the B Company detachment, while you will command the expedition. You will also take one of the two Gatling guns that we have at this post. You will take two wagons for ammunition and one for hospital and similar supplies. Your men will carry such field and emergency rations as you can. For the rest of your food you will have to depend upon the country through which you will pass. I am sorry for this, but on a swift, hard-fighting expedition a command the size of yours cannot be burdened with more wagons."

"That is true," spoke Captain Freeman thoughtfully. "Well, we shall have to do the best we can with the amount of transport and rations that you can put at our disposal. I am anxious now, sir, to get started with the preparations as rapidly as possible."

"Good; it is half-past nine now. You should be ready to march by——"

"By half-past eleven at the latest," supplied Captain Freeman, rising.

Never were preparations more rushed, nor yet more thoroughly made.

First of all, it was necessary to send into Bantoc and recall Lieutenant Holmes and the guard stationed there. With the removal of the troops the lives of the white people residing in Bantoc would be in immediate danger. So the twenty-five or thirty white residents were obliged to accompany the guard out to Fort Benjamin Franklin, where they were to be provided with temporary quarters.

Ten minutes before the time named by Captain Freeman all had been accomplished. The column was ready and started.

B Company's detachment marched first. Behind this came the transport wagons and the Gatling gun. The C Company detachment, under Lieutenant Greg Holmes, brought up the rear.

Taking into account those who had lately been killed and wounded, and also the guard under Sergeant Dinsmore, left out at the Seaforth plantation, Captain Cortland had remaining as a garrison about sixty effective soldiers. These must preserve the safety of the post and the order of Bantoc through the twenty-four hours of each day.

No soldier in the marching column deluded himself with the belief that he was starting on a brief expedition. Every man knew that it would be weeks before they were likely to set eyes again on Fort Franklin. It was, moreover, wholly probable that some of the soldiers now marching would never see the fort again.

Yet officers and men tramped away unconcernedly. All acted, and felt, very much as though this had been merely a practice march through a peaceful country.

Noll Terry was jubilant. Hal had seen active service on this island, and now his chum was about to do the same thing. The first taste of real service is always dear to the heart of a good soldier.

Night brought the command within three or four miles of the foot of the mountains. The next morning was still young when the column wound its way up into the lower portion of the mountains.

Captain Freeman was not marching blindly. He was provided with military maps of the mountains. Then, again, not all the Moros were hostile to the Americans. There were many friendly natives, and some of them had slyly brought word to the post of the location of Datto Hakkut and his forces at the last report.

As to the number of men with the datto, the statements of the natives had varied. They had estimated the datto's force at all the way from fifteen hundred to twenty-five hundred fighting men. Captains Cortland and Freeman, with their knowledge of the native tendency to exaggerate, had thus fixed the probable number at about eight hundred men.

The second and the third days passed. The troops were now far up in the mountains, though up to that time they had not encountered the enemy. Captain Freeman, however, pushed forward, feeling confident that he would sooner or later encounter the datto's forces.

On the fourth morning, an hour after daylight, the troops were again under way. They moved slowly, for the roads were in bad condition and the column could not go ahead at greater speed than the transport wagons could maintain.

A "point" was out in advance, followed by a slightly larger advance guard. Behind marched a watchful rear guard. The little column, for its own safety and convenience, was strung out over a goodly length of road.

As Lieutenant Prescott passed, Sergeant Noll Terry stepped out and saluted.

"What is it, Sergeant?"

"If it is proper, I would like the lieutenant's permission to go up ahead and walk with Sergeant Overton."

"That will be all right, Sergeant—if you will remember that, in case of emergency, you are to return hastily to your proper place in the line."

"Thank you; I will, sir."

"Very good, Sergeant."

Once more saluting, Noll hastened up forward.

"You have a message?" asked Hal.

"No; but I have the lieutenant's permission to walk with you."

"I'm glad of it, chum. Talking makes the walking easier."

"Walking—yes," grumbled Noll. "I'm afraid that's about all we're going to get out of this hike."

"Never pray for a fight, Noll. It's all right when it has to be, but any real fight always means the last hour for some good fellows."

"I'm no hog for a fight," grunted Terry, "but I'd like to have just a little real practice, after the long, long time I've had to put in preparing for it."

"Hm!" smiled Sergeant Hal. "I could almost qualify as a member of a peace society. *I* don't care how long it is before the next fight. I'd hate to see it come along this stretch of road."

"Why?"

"Well, look over at our left, Noll. Below us is a deep gully, with a swift stream flowing. Beyond it is that wooded ledge. Any number of Moros could conceal themselves there and fire at us, and we couldn't reach 'em with the bayonet. Ahead——"

Sergeant Hal may have finished, but, if he did, his voice was drowned out by the savage clamor of yells ahead. Barely a hundred yards beyond the point came a rushing mob of Moros, shooting and brandishing creeses.

From the wooded, inaccessible ledge to the left came a sudden, rapid firing that made the air hot with bullets directed at Uncle Sam's men.

CHAPTER XIX

HAL TURNS THE GATLING GUN LOOSE

"Gatling gun to the head of the line! Lie down, men!"

Two men dropped even before the order had been given, for Moro bullets had found them.

After firing volleys, the "point" and advance guard fell back on the run.

"Take the infantry fire at this point, Sergeant Overton!" commanded Lieutenant Prescott briskly.

"Open magazines! Load magazines!" shouted Sergeant Hal to the men in the swiftly formed front rank. "Ready, aim! At will, point-blank range—fire!"

Prettily enough the American fire opened on the Moros rushing down the narrow path.

The centre of the American column, at Lieutenant Holmes's order, opened fire across the gully at the wooded ambush on the left.

Captain Freeman took up his stand a little forward of the centre, where he could watch the fire in both directions.

"Hurry up that Gatling gun, Prescott."

"Yes, sir."

Prescott and two privates were working at lightning speed to get the Gatling placed. Then the lieutenant fed in a belt of ammunition.

"Sergeant Terry, relieve Sergeant Overton in charge of the advancing firing line. Overton, come here."

"Yes, sir," responded Hal, running up and saluting.

Lieutenant Prescott was just finishing the sighting of the Gatling.

"Attend to the firing of this piece, Sergeant. Fire steadily, though not at fullest speed. Keep it going continuously until it becomes too hot, or until I give the word to stop."

"Very good, sir."

"Begin firing, Sergeant."

Hal's answer was to turn the firing mechanism loose.

R-r-r-r-rip! rang out the exploding cartridges too rapidly for count. Hal swung the nose of the piece slightly from side to side, and the storm of Gatling bullets raked thoroughly the road ahead.

At first the on-rushing Moros had been almost stopped by the sudden, low, accurate infantry fire. They were to be seen ahead in great force, and the cries of their leaders drove them on with greater steadiness.

Now, as the crackling of the Gatling rose on the air, and its projectiles swept the road ahead, constantly supported by brisk infantry fire from at least forty men, the natives were forced to halt. Then they wavered. The hoarse, taunting cries of their leaders, however, drove them forward again.

Twice they wavered, under the blistering fire of the regulars, though each time their leaders succeeded in driving the brown men forward again.

When the fight opened there were at least six hundred yelling Moros in sight, but they were now dropping by scores.

Then, with a wild yell, three hundred more rushed around the base of a low hill, joining the assailants.

"Are the Moros cowards?" demanded the deep, penetrating voice of one of the leaders. "Are the Moros women, that they would live forever? Has heaven no joys for the faithful that you would remain so long away?"

That stirred the fanatical blood of the brown men. They were equal to anything, now! On they dashed, though the Gatling and the steady infantry fire withered the ranks in advance.

On they came, disdaining, now, to return rifle fire with rifle fire. Over their own dead and wounded stepped the brown men, and rushed on.

"Cease firing there, Sergeant Terry. Give 'em the steel!" bellowed Lieutenant Prescott hoarsely, using his hands for a trumpet, though he stood barely twelve feet from young Terry.

"Cease firing," Noll repeated squarely in the bugler's ear. Then the notes of the bugle arose, clear and loud. The firing died out.

"It's cold steel, men! Fix bayonets!" shouted Sergeant Noll.

But Sergeant Hal and two men had dragged the Gatling, momentarily silenced, to one side of the road, where they could still employ this machine of destruction.

Another belt of cartridges Sergeant Overton fed in. Then he started the machine again.

R-r-r-r-rip! The Gatling was performing at hand-to-hand quarters now. Noll sent a dozen men to stand by the gun, defending it from capture with their lives.

Clash! Zing! Slash! Slash! Thrust—cut! It was steel against steel now. On more open ground the Moros might have had a slight advantage, for they are skilled users of the sword and creese, and when their blood is up they know little in the way of terror.

R-r-r-r-rip! It was the Gatling, at such close quarters, that now dismayed the brown men. With no mean quality of heroism, they threw themselves against the gun's defenders. They would seize that demon of machinery and hurl it over into the gully below. But the doughboys, with bayonets stationed on the sides of the gun, thrust or stabbed them back. No native approached the muzzle of the Gatling and lived to cause further trouble. In as wide an arc as possible Sergeant Hal swung the nose of the piece from side to side.

Private Danton, standing close to Hal, ready to feed in the next belt of cartridges, fell with a Moro bullet in his brain. Another soldier sprang forward, snatched up the belt of ammunition and stood ready to feed.

Fully twenty-five hundred rounds of Gatling ammunition were thus fired into the dense brown ranks before the Moros felt that they could endure it no longer. On that narrow road they had failed to reach the piece itself. Four brown sharpshooters, back in the ranks, had been detailed by a Moro officer to climb a tree and fill with lead the body of the indomitable young sergeant. As the bullets sang past his head, Hal discovered the tree, turned the Gatling muzzle that way, and fairly shot the leaves off a portion of it. Two of the sharpshooters dropped, riddled through. The other pair dropped from sheer terror.

Sergeant Hal Swung the Nose of the Gun from Side to Side.

Now that the execution on that narrow mountain road was becoming more than flesh and blood could stand, the Moros broke in pell-mell confusion.

"Forward, there, Lieutenant Prescott!" yelled Captain Freeman. "Give 'em the bayonet. But don't let your men get away from you."

Prescott's answer was conveyed only by a wave of his stick. After the fleeing Moros he rushed his men, and the Malays in the rear received many an ugly wound.

"Keep the Gatling close up with the advance, Sergeant!" ordered Captain Freeman, striding forward.

When the Moros in front had gotten to hand-to-hand quarters the flanking fire from across the gully had ceased, after having killed two of Freeman's men and wounding six more. Now it reopened.

"Halt, Sergeant! Swing that Gatling around. Turn it loose across the gully."

R-r-r-r-rip! Captain Freeman sent two men back on the run to bring up more ammunition for the machine gun. Within two minutes the fire from across the gully had ceased. In the meantime three more regulars of the centre had been hit.

"Now, run it forward, Sergeant," commanded Captain Freeman. "Support Lieutenant Prescott. The Moros have halted him for the moment."

Again the Gatling went into action up front, where Sergeant Noll Terry, in the front rank, was taking more than his share of the attack, though as yet he had given many wounds and received none. Yet Prescott's advance would have been driven back had it not been for the prompt arrival of the machine gun.

The transport and rear guard were coming up now.

"Corporal," called Captain Freeman, "my compliments to Lieutenant Prescott, and tell him that I want the whole line to move forward as rapidly as possible. Our only safety, now, lies in getting as quickly as possible off this road and into an open country."

Prescott received the order, and right loyally responded. As often as possible the Gatling, now up with the advance, was given an opportunity to cool.

Within twenty minutes after the opening of the attack the Moro spirit was broken for the time. They had had more than a hundred men killed and wounded, and that was all the brown men could stand for the first onset.

"Don't pursue any further," ordered Captain Freeman, well up with the advance by this time. "Let the rascals get away if they don't interfere with our advance. We'll have them at hand to fight when we're ready, Lieutenant. What we must do now is to get a place where we can fortify ourselves and look after our wounded."

"We've a heavy list, I fear, sir."

"Heavy enough," replied Captain Freeman gravely.

There was no further opposition to the advance of the regulars, who, despite the great inferiority of their numbers, had made the brown men respect their fighting grit and prowess. Within ten minutes after Captain Freeman's order to abandon the chase there was no visible evidence that there were any Moros in the neighboring mountains.

"March to the right, and take that hill yonder in quick time, Lieutenant Prescott," directed Captain Freeman.

"Very good, sir."

"Follow the lieutenant, you men with the Gatling," ordered the commanding officer, and Hal and his comrades covered the ground as quickly as they could. No opposition was offered to their taking the hill. Here the first regulars to arrive dropped down panting, though Prescott, Hal and Noll remained standing and vigilant. Slowly the rest of the column climbed the hill. After a brief rest the men were set to work fortifying the crest of this little rise of ground.

No trench is ever dug, by a wise commander, at the exact top of a hill, but always at a point a little below, which is called the "military crest." If the trench were on the top of the hill, every time the men raised themselves to fire, their heads and trunks would stand out too clearly defined against the sky-line, and make them easy marks for an enemy below.

Up on the top of the hill, however, was a depression in the ground. Into this space the transport wagons were driven, and here the dead were laid out and the wounded attended to.

A deadly morning's work it had proved. Five infantrymen had been killed, twelve were wounded badly enough to be out of the fighting lists for the present, while twenty-two others, though more or less wounded, were still fit for duty.

"Now, chum, you see what follows the fighting," murmured Hal in Noll's ear. "How do you like what follows the fighting?"

"It looks some grim," Sergeant Terry admitted, wrapping his left hand where a creese had made a gash. "But what are we here for, and why are we soldiers, if this sort of thing doesn't appeal to us?"

"I'm afraid you're hopelessly blood-thirsty," smiled Hal.

"No; I'm not. I enlisted because I believed I'd like the soldier life, and fighting is the highest expression of the soldier's work."

"Hello, there, 'Long'!" called Private Kelly.

"Yes?" answered Private William Green, turning at the hail.

"Did you bring along your kantab and pass plenty of it to the goo-goos?"

"I'll make no money here," grunted William disdaining to answer Kelly's teasing question. "There's no chance to spend money here, so none of the fellows will borrow from me."

"Making no money?" Kelly rebuked him. "Man, isn't your government pay running along, and ain't ye glad ye're here to be drawing it?"

"I don't like this fighting business," grumbled Slosson.

"Why not?" inquired Kelly in mild surprise.

"In that hike I lost my pipe. Lucky for me I brought two more along in my pack. I'll get one of them out, now. Want the other, Kelly?"

"I do not, lad, and my thanks to you. Slosson, I'm beginning to think we ought to force the brown men to accept pipes. If they smoked 'em the way you do yours there'd soon be fewer of the pesky brown goo-goos in this land."

CHAPTER XX
CORPORAL DUXBRIDGE'S MISTAKE

Fortunately there was water, a clear, cool spring of it just below the trench line. As soon as the men were rested, Captain Freeman detailed a score of them to haul water up into camp.

"Don't get into groups, you water carriers, either," Lieutenant Prescott called after the men as they started down the slope with buckets. "Keep apart. If you don't, some of the Moros in the distance will be taking pot-shots and getting some of you."

The day wore on, and it looked as though the Moros were still running.

"I'd hate to have to take ten men and fight all of the enemy who are within two thousand yards of here," declared Captain Freeman in the hearing of a large part of his command. "The datto has us all in a bunch and he'll hang to us until he has wiped us out."

"I don't believe he can do it, sir," retorted Lieutenant Greg Holmes.

"No; but the brown rascal thinks he can, which amounts to the same thing as far as he is concerned. Mr. Holmes, you may safely take my word for it that the datto has made up his own mind not to allow one of us ever to get back in safety to Bantoc."

Late in the afternoon the five soldiers who had been slain were placed in a row at the top of the hill.

"Too bad we haven't a Flag to drape the poor fellows with," said Captain Freeman sorrowfully.

"We have a Flag with us, sir," spoke up Hal, saluting.

"Where is it, Sergeant?"

"In a small parcel in one of the ammunition wagons, sir."

"How does it happen to be there, Sergeant?"

"I put it in myself, sir. It's the Flag that the Moros hauled down from the flagstaff over the schoolhouse near Seaforth's—the Flag they slashed and danced upon. I picked it up at that time, sir; and when we started on this expedition I placed the Flag in one of the wagons."

"Why did you do that, Sergeant?"

"Because I was in hopes that before we get through with this expedition, sir, we'd find a chance to make Datto Hakkut and his men salute the American Flag."

"Bring the Flag here, Sergeant."

Hal brought it, and its tattered folds were so laid that some remnant of the bunting touched each of the five bodies of the slain soldiers.

Assembling half his command, while the other half watched in the trenches, Captain Freeman read the prayers and the service for the dead. Three volleys were fired over the graves after the slain men had been laid in them. Bugler Swanson blew "taps," after which the graves were carefully filled and the tops sodded so that roving Moros would not afterwards find and desecrate these graves, sacred to the American people. All in good time the American military authorities would send and exhume these remains, transferring them to marked resting places in military cemeteries.

Before supper Captain Freeman summoned his two officers in council with him.

"I want to talk with you young gentlemen," began the captain, "for the reason that, of course, by the fortunes of war, I may be removed at any moment. If anything happens to me Mr. Prescott is to be regarded as ranking officer. Now, I want you both to understand my plan in taking up my position on this hill. Do either of you guess it?"

"I think I do, sir," replied Lieutenant Prescott, after a pause.

"Very good, Mr. Prescott. What is my reason?"

"You were sent out, sir, to meet Datto Hakkut, fight him and disperse his forces."

"Exactly," nodded the captain.

"This hill, sir, will be a hard nut for the brown men to crack. If he hopes to do it, Hakkut must get every available fighting man here on the spot."

"You're right," nodded Freeman.

"Thus, sir, you hope to force Hakkut to concentrate his whole fighting force in this immediate country. If you get all the rascals in front of you you'll have them all in one lot to whip."

"You've fathomed my plan very easily, Mr. Prescott, and you've exactly stated it. Now, though I shall take pains to be sure that the Moros remain in this neighborhood, I shall not force any very hard fighting for two or three days. Our rations will last longer than that, with care. After I've given Hakkut time enough to get his whole crew together then I shall go after them as hard as I can considering the size of this force. Also, by waiting, we shall give several of our wounded men time to get back into fighting condition."

"But what, sir," broke in Lieutenant Holmes, "if the datto takes your negative course for a confession of weakness, and attempts to carry this hill by assault?"

"Answer that, if you can, Mr. Prescott," directed Captain Freeman, turning to the other West Pointer.

"Why, I imagine, sir, that you hope your seeming inactivity *will* provoke Hakkut into trying to carry this hill by assault. This hill, defended by regulars, will be no easy place to take from us, and Hakkut will lose so many of his men that the experience will be a good lesson for him."

"That's the idea," nodded the commanding officer. "Now, gentlemen, you understand the plan thus far. But there's another important point to remember. If we are cooped up here for very many days, then the men will have nothing left to eat but grass and gravel. So you will understand that, presently, it is going to be a matter of prime necessity for us to be able to leave here and forage. Therefore, during our comparative inactivity, we must provoke Hakkut into as many assaults as possible upon this position. The more attempts he makes the more his fighting men will be demoralized when we at last fight our way through his lines."

During that night no attack was made, and the men had little to do beyond carrying out guard duty. Hakkut had undoubtedly dispatched messengers to bring all possible fighting men to the scene.

Nor in the morning, even two hours after daylight, was there any sign of the enemy. Captain Freeman at last took up his field glass again and intently studied a deep forest some twelve hundred yards below.

"Sergeant Overton!"

"Sir?"

"Have the Gatling and a belt of ammunition brought up."

"Very good, sir."

When the Gatling had been placed, Captain Freeman handed his glass to the young sergeant.

"Overton, look through the glass and see if you can discover the line of timber that I'm going to describe to you."

Hal very soon had the spot located.

"Now, Sergeant, sight the Gatling for twelve hundred yards. Do it carefully. When you are ready do what you can to stir up life along that line of timber."

While Sergeant Hal was making ready, Captain Freeman remained attentively watching the timber line through his glass.

R-r-r-r-r-rip! Hal served with speed and intensity.

"Just as I thought!" exclaimed the commanding officer. "You've got a line of brown men on the nervous jump down there. Keep it up a little longer, Sergeant. Sweep over a wider area."

Then, after a pause:

"Cease firing."

For an hour Captain Freeman let the enemy rest. He was watching other points through his glass. At last he ordered the Gatling into action again. The trick was played a third time that morning, and each time some of the Moros were disturbed.

"That's one of the things I wanted to know," remarked Captain Freeman at last. "Hakkut has this camp completely surrounded, but is keeping his men quiet. I wish we had two or three more Gatlings and a whole wagon load of this special ammunition. We could make it interesting for the goo-goos."

However, the datto made no move to attack, though Captain Freeman believed that the rebel, by this time, must have twelve hundred fighting men, at least, in the forests below.

"Hakkut may realize the difficulty of assaulting us here, and may be waiting for huge reinforcements," Captain Freeman confided to his two lieutenants. "Moreover, I think it extremely likely that we have been caught underestimating the force of the enemy."

"There's one good thing about this style of campaigning, sir," smiled Prescott, "It isn't eating up any more men in casualties."

"No; but the datto is figuring that he's letting us eat up our rations."

There were no attacks that afternoon or evening. The next morning Captain Freeman hesitated as to whether or not he should send out a party in force to "locate and develop" the enemy. But he decided not to do so.

"To-morrow, though," declared the captain to his lieutenants, "we'll break through the line somewhere."

That third night Sergeant Hal was placed in charge of the guard, with Lieutenant Greg Holmes as his direct superior. On the side of camp where the commanding officer thought the enemy most numerous, Hal placed Corporal Duxbridge in charge.

"Don't close your eyes to-night, Corporal," warned the young sergeant. "You can get your sleep in the daytime. This is the point where the greatest vigilance is needed. This point is really the key to the camp, and every man who lies down to sleep to-night leaves his life in your hands."

"All right," replied Corporal Duxbridge in a voice that sounded weary.

"You'll be sure to keep awake?"

"I know my business, Sergeant."

Hal Overton did not particularly like Duxbridge. He belonged to C Company, and was a man subject to occasional fits of crankiness. But Duxbridge, as well as the others, had his share of duty to perform.

Late that night one of the men of the guard, stationed not far from Duxbridge, thought that he heard a slight noise down the slope. He listened only a moment, then felt sure that he had espied a figure crawling along further down the slope.

"Halt!" called the soldier. "Halt or I'll fire. Who's there?"

"A friend," came the answer in perfectly good English. "For Heaven's sake don't fire. We've had enough of horrors with the fiends below. Where's Corporal Duxbridge? He knows me."

"Corporal Duxbridge is on duty at this point," returned the soldier. "How many of you are there?"

"Seven; but I will come up alone first and speak with the corporal."

Duxbridge was called quietly. The corporal had been dozing for twenty minutes, and he awoke with mind somewhat befogged.

The stranger below, who had been allowed to advance, now stepped up to where the corporal could scrutinize him.

"Why, I know this man," declared the corporal. "His name's Eusebio Davo. He's a wealthy Tagalo, loyal to the government and a good man. What's the trouble, Señor Davo?"

"Corporal, I went south in the island to pick up some laborers from the Manobo tribe. I got forty together and was on my way through this country, not knowing that the Moros were out. So we were caught, this afternoon, and taken before the Datto Hakkut. He ordered us into his ranks to fight. We demurred, and four of my fellows were cut down before my eyes. Then we accepted arms. But to-night we tried to creep through the datto's lines and get here. All but the six men with me were caught, and their fate must have been awful."

Señor Davo shuddered, then went on:

"I come to beseech you that you allow my poor fellows to come inside your lines. You know me, Corporal, and know that we're all right."

"Yes, bring your men inside our line," decided Corporal Duxbridge. "I'll vouch for you, Señor Davo, to our commanding officer."

Protesting his undying gratitude, Davo went below for his men, and brought them inside the lines, a sorry looking lot of fellows who at once threw themselves down as if to sleep.

"You'll notify Sergeant Overton, of course?" suggested the soldier who had first halted Davo.

"You mind your business, Strong," Corporal Duxbridge rebuked him. "I'll notify the sergeant in good time."

But Hal, as it happened, was nearer than had been imagined. Unobserved he had listened to the whole conversation. Now, Overton hastened silently away, awaking Lieutenant Holmes and ten soldiers. Without undue haste these marched down on Duxbridge's station.

"Halt! Who goes there?"

"The officer of the day and the sergeant of the guard," came the response, in Lieutenant Holmes's crisp tones.

"Advance, sir."

The seven new arrivals lay on the ground, apparently sound asleep. Davo had his hat over his face, and was snoring lightly.

"Who are these new men in camp, Corporal?" demanded Holmes sharply.

"Fugitives from the datto's lines, sir. I was about to notify the sergeant of the guard, sir."

"Don't let them get away," spoke Hal quickly to the men, "and remember that they're armed with steel! This fellow, who calls himself Davo is Vicente Tomba, a Tagalo who is right-hand man to the datto," added the sergeant, bending and snatching the hat from the Tagalo's face.

It was truly Tomba, who, with a snarl, leaped to his feet ere Hal Overton could grab him.

"Shoot him!" ordered Lieutenant Holmes, as Tomba went over the trench and down the slope at sprinting speed. Three or four rifles spoke, but Tomba escaped in the darkness.

Not so, however, with the men Tomba had brought with him. Not one of them escaped. All were stretched on the ground senseless, having been clubbed with the butts of the soldiers' rifles. Then, a quick search under the shirt of each of the rascals, revealed a creese with blade ground to a razor edge.

"You see, Corporal," ripped out Sergeant Hal, "these scoundrels were going to watch their chance to knife you all in the dark. Then the Moros would have rushed in at this point, and——"

Hal's prediction was verified, at that instant, by the breaking out of a fiendish chorus of yells down the slope. The Moros, waiting below, were advancing to a night attack.

"Bugler of the guard! Sound the general alarm!" roared out Lieutenant Holmes's steady tones.

CHAPTER XXI

SCOUTING IN DEADLY EARNEST

It was a ferocious attack, promptly and staunchly met.

Soldiers in the field on campaign sleep in their full clothing, their rifles at their sides. It takes not more than ten seconds to turn a soldier out in the night, fully awake and ready for orders. The knowledge that their lives depend upon their promptness keeps the men in condition for quick obedience.

Even the Gatling was ready at the top of the hill. From point to point it was dragged, and wherever it was served the midnight assailants soon drew back.

For twenty minutes the conflict was kept up, often at closest quarters. But at last the sounding of the Moro horns in the rear called off the assailants, who fled in the darkness.

"How did this all happen, Mr. Holmes?" asked Captain Freeman. "I must congratulate you on being alert and ready for the brown men."

"Sergeant Overton had just called me, sir. And I think you will wish to hear what he has to say."

Hal was sent for and reported instantly.

"I know, now, sir, why Tomba wanted to make my acquaintance, and that of Sergeant Terry, sir," Hal explained, and then told what had happened.

"How did Corporal Duxbridge ever happen to do a thing like that?" demanded Freeman angrily.

"Tomba had already made the Corporal's acquaintance, sir. Tomba wanted to make mine, and Terry's, as soon as he knew the Thirty-fourth was coming to these southern islands. It was Tomba's belief that he could run a gang of creese men past us, and get inside where he could knife the nearest soldiers, and then let an attacking party in."

"If the Moros had ever gotten through our line they'd have wiped the camp out to-night," exclaimed Captain Freeman.

"Of course they would, sir, and that is the way in which Tomba, even in Manila, had planned to make our acquaintance, and use it for just such an undertaking as to-night's. It seems, sir, that having failed with us, he succeeded in getting on the right side of Corporal Duxbridge."

"Where, I wonder?" muttered the captain. "And where is the Corporal?"

"Just taken up above with the wounded, sir," replied Lieutenant Holmes. "Corporal Duxbridge was hit, sir."

"Let us go up to see him. Where are the six natives?"

"Tied, sir, and up with the wounded."

Corporal Duxbridge, when the commanding officer visited him, felt sheepish enough, despite the great pain he was in. He now readily explained how Tomba, under the assumed name of Davo, had made his acquaintance in Bantoc. Tomba had spent money so freely in entertaining him that Duxbridge had been certain that the man must be a wealthy, good-natured Tagalo.

"I hope you've learned a lesson, Corporal," said Captain Freeman sadly. "You're one of five wounded in to-night's performance, and two of our finest men are dead."

Corporal Duxbridge covered his face with his hands.

"I was a big fool," he confessed brokenly.

There were no more attacks that night, but in the morning the Moros developed a new style of trouble. All through the day, from one point or another, they kept the American trenches under fire at frequent intervals. Captain Freeman, however, refused to allow his men to waste ammunition. They must not fire until the brown men attempted an assault.

That night only half rations were served to the defenders of the hill. There was but little food left. During the night there were three assaults against the force on the hill, though none of them were desperately fought.

"Hakkut is going to adopt a new trick of keeping us awake day and night," muttered Captain Freeman grimly.

The next day there was more annoying firing against the trenches, though the Moros had learned their lesson too well to attempt any rushes during daylight.

Just after dark, that evening, Captain Freeman sent for his officers. He also allowed Hal and Noll and two sergeants from C Company to be on hand to hear the discussion.

"To-morrow night, at the latest, we've got to fight our way out of here," announced Captain Freeman. "To remain here later than to-morrow night will be to invite starvation—which, in our position, means nothing less than destruction. I fear, too, that we shall be obliged to abandon our transport wagons. Our wounded we can carry on stretchers made with poles and blankets. There must be some point in the Moro line where we can break through—some point so weakly guarded that we can be on our way before the brown rascals can gather in force enough to put up a hard fight. This fact can be determined only through the work of a scouting party."

"I shall be delighted, sir, to volunteer for scouting duty," spoke up Lieutenant Prescott.

"And I also, sir," added Lieutenant Holmes.

"Thank you. I knew that you would both be ready," replied the commanding officer. "Yet we must remember that, while our scouts are out to-night, this camp is also extremely liable to attack. If the latter be the case, I do not see how I can spare either of my officers. Now, I have cause to remember a time when, in the mountains of Colorado, when on practice field duty, two of our non-commissioned officers especially distinguished themselves as scouts. I believe that both of the young men still possess that ability in marked degree. It seems to me that the choice of a leader for a scouting party lies between Sergeants Overton and Terry."

"Thank you, sir," broke in Sergeant Hal gravely. "May I suggest, sir, that there is no need of making a choice between us? I would like to go on this duty, sir, and I'd rather have Sergeant Terry with me than any other enlisted man in the regiment."

"I'm ready, sir," declared Noll promptly.

"It seems almost foolish to allow two such excellent sergeants to go," returned Captain Freeman gravely. "You see, we need as good men in the camp as we do outside of it. However, let it be as you wish, Sergeant Overton. How many men do you think you will need with you?"

"None, sir, except Sergeant Terry," spoke Hal.

"Are two enough for safety, Sergeant, in your opinion."

"Two men are safer than a dozen on scouting duty, I think, sir. Two men can get through in places where even four men would be caught at it."

"But if caught, two are a small number for defensive purposes."

"There won't be much defense possible, sir, if we're caught; but I think Sergeant Terry agrees with me that we ought not to be caught."

"Will you take your rifle and bayonet, Sergeant?"

"I'd rather not, sir. In fact, the plan that has come into my mind at this moment is for Sergeant Terry and myself to stain our faces and bodies with juice from the berries of the boka bush that is growing inside our lines. Then we'll rob two of the native prisoners of their clothing, under which we can each carry a service revolver and a creese. That is, sir, if you approve my plan."

Captain Freeman was silent for some moments.

"I'm afraid you're planning an especially desperate undertaking, Sergeant Overton. I quite understand your idea in dressing like natives. But if you are seen, you will be spoken to. It will be in the native tongue. What then? You can't answer in native speech."

"But I think, sir," argued Hal, "that you'll agree that there are probably men from several tribes under the datto's command. In that case many different tribal dialects will be spoken. Noll—pardon me, sir—Sergeant Terry and I can answer in any heathen-sounding, guttural sort of words, and look stupid."

"It's quite difficult, my lad, to improvise a pretended language on the spur of the moment."

"Hakka kado me no tonga, lakka prada estig ferente," rejoined Hal Overton, with a grin.

"Dikka mone peditti u nono mate ben," said Noll cheerfully.

"What language is that, lads?" demanded Captain Freeman.

"New Jersey hog-Latin, I imagine, sir," replied Sergeant Hal soberly.

"I do not believe, gentlemen, that we can send better scouts than Sergeants Overton and Terry," said Captain Freeman.

His two subordinates expressed their agreement.

"Sergeants, you may go and prepare yourselves. Do it as speedily as you can, and report to me as soon as you are ready."

There was sullen objection from two of the native prisoners, when their clothing was taken from them. Hal and Noll, however, loaned their blankets in exchange.

"You know, Noll, if we don't succeed to-night, we shall have no further use for our blankets, anyway," Hal remarked dryly.

"I've thought of that," Sergeant Terry nodded.

After they had dyed their skin and hair with the juice of the boka the two Army boys next distributed a liberal amount of dirt on themselves, then drew on the borrowed clothing, consisting only of shirts and short trousers. Inside their clothing each tucked a sharp-edged creese, also a loaded service revolver.

"You'll do, in the dark," nodded Captain Freeman, after looking them over keenly. "Of course, you won't show yourselves in a strong light, anyway. Now, you don't need instructions. You understand your errand."

Captain Freeman himself took the two Army boys through the darkness to the trench.

"I am turning these fellows loose, men," the captain announced. "But don't allow any of the others to go through the lines."

To the captain's relief, the disguises appeared to "work" well in the dark, for the men on guard in the trench merely saluted.

CHAPTER XXII
PLAYING GOO-GOO IN A GRIM GAME

Down the slope the Army boys walked boldly for a few hundred yards. The night was so dark that there was small possibility of being seen at a distance.

"Now, we'd better go a little more cautiously," whispered Hal, checking his companion by a touch on the arm.

"It's going to rain within a very few minutes," Noll whispered in return, as he looked up at the inky sky overhead.

"The more rain the better. I hope there will be no lightning."

"Where are you going to try to slip through the lines?"

"Do you remember the gully that runs back through the woods below, somewhat to our left as we stand now?" queried Hal.

"Yes; certainly."

"That gully is a trap such as sane soldiers would hardly dare venture into. If they did, and were discovered, the Moros could annihilate them from above."

"Surely," nodded Noll.

"Therefore I have an idea that the Moros haven't attempted to guard that gully in force, though there may be men on either side above it. Noll, if we are careful not to make a sound I think we can steal through that gully without getting caught."

"Or else we'll run into a hundred times as much trouble as we can handle," replied Noll thoughtfully.

"It's worth taking a chance, isn't it?"

"I think it's the best single chance I can see."

"Come along, then," whispered Hal. "You might keep just a little behind me. I think I can find the mouth of the gully, even in this pitchy blackness. If you see me drop to my knees, do the same."

Hal started forward again. The natural-born scout, once he has observed a place in the daylight, has some kind of an instinct that guides him to the same spot in the darkness.

Sergeant Hal had not gone far when the rain began to descend. There were distant rumblings of thunder, but no lightning. For this he was thankful. He hoped to be behind the Moro lines before lightning began to flash.

Two wanderers in front of the enemy's lines would be sure to excite suspicion, while two seeming natives behind the lines would attract little attention.

Presently Sergeant Overton dropped to his knees, peering ahead and listening keenly, as he crept along. Sergeant Terry imitated his chum. Hal crawled within fifty feet of the mouth of the gully, just a little south of it. After a moment's pause he obtained his bearings and extended one arm in silent direction to Noll.

Then they crept noiselessly into the mouth of the gully. So far they had not been hailed, but this was not positive proof that human eyes were not watching their movements.

Once inside the gully they moved, cautiously, still on hands and knees, halting after every advance of two or three feet. They were shivering in their thin raiment, for the rain was heavy and cold. Noll's teeth were all but chattering.

"I don't believe the gully is guarded at all," whispered young Overton in his friend's ear. "This place looks so like a trap that few military commanders would ever think of leading men into it in the dark. I figure that the datto thought this gully not worth guarding by night."

"The slopes above us on either side may be well guarded, however," warned Noll.

"Yes; and you can wager that we'll know all about that before we try to go back to camp," returned Hal. "The place to start such an investigation is from the rear of the enemy's lines."

"All right; lead on."

They had gone another hundred feet into the gully when Hal Overton stopped again. Now he rose to his feet.

"We'll walk through," he whispered. "I don't believe we will run into any of the datto's men hereabouts. If we do, leave it to me to do the first talking."

"Jersey hog-Latin?" queried Noll, with a grin.

"Of course; Spanish or English would be fatal to fellows who look the part that we're rigged up to play."

Hal walked on, steadily, though with caution. Noll kept a few feet behind him until the gully widened, then stepped to his chum's side.

Neither spoke. There was danger in unnecessary conversation. They had covered six hundred feet more when they felt, rather than saw, that they were nearing the further end of the gully.

At last they stepped out into the open—then received a sudden shock. Less than a dozen feet away a Moro sentry, rifle on shoulder, halted, regarding them keenly.

"Manu batto dobi kem," murmured Hal to his chum, in a low voice. Noll answered in the same low tone. Both were shaking with more than the chill of the rain, but Hal turned to the sentry, inquiring mildly:

"Hoppo tuti sen antrim mak?"

The Moro sentry shook his head. He did not understand that dialect.

"Basta morti hengo pas tum," murmured Hal regretfully, hesitating before the sentry.

"Manga tim no troka," remarked Noll.

Hal turned slowly, nodding at his chum. Then both strolled along, the sentry merely staring after them.

"That's the advantage of scouting within the lines of an enemy where many tongues are spoken," whispered Noll in his chum's ear.

The Army boys had not gone twenty feet, however, when they ran into another Moro sentry, who stood under a tree evidently trying to keep out of the rain.

This sentry addressed them with two or three words in the Moro tongue.

"Banda nokku him slengo mat," replied Hal.

Again the sentry spoke to them, accompanying his words with a gesture that seemed to order them to pass on. The Army boys were glad enough to obey.

"We're right in the middle of the hornet's nest," whispered Noll.

Fifty feet further on the Army boys came upon a rudely built shack under which a number of brown men were huddled to escape the rain.

"The outpost crowd," whispered Hal. "Noll, I believe we're getting into the heart of the Moros' camp."

Noll was about to answer, but at that moment discerning another sentry, a few yards ahead, checked his reply. This sentinel they managed to pass without words. Being well within the enemy's lines now, and apparently natives themselves, the Army boys were not as likely to attract suspicion to themselves.

A heavier downpour of rain drove the young scouts for a moment under the spreading branches of a large tree.

"This job is almost as easy as stealing the marmalade from mother's preserve closet," chuckled Sergeant Noll, despite his discomfort.

"This place is like a good many traps," replied Hal. "It seems easy enough to get in, but remember, boy, we've got to get out."

As soon as the rain slackened somewhat the two scouts sauntered on again. Here and there they passed rude shacks in which Moros and allied natives were sleeping. Then the young scouts came upon a new scene that made them fairly catch their breath.

They were standing by a mud wall now, a wall of about nine feet in height. There could be no doubt that this was a Moro fort, erected for a particular purpose, and Hal's active mind immediately fathomed that purpose.

"The datto's own headquarters!" he whispered in his chum's ear. "Oh, Noll, I hope that I am right!"

Terry nodded. He was as excited as was his comrade.

The wall, as well as the Army boys could judge, was more than two hundred feet long. About half way down they came to a gate. Here six Moro sentries, armed with rifles and protected from the storm by woven rush raincoats, stood on guard.

Hal boldly stepped nearer, for the sentries were already regarding this straying pair of natives. Noll, with a quick catch in his throat, stepped after his chum. It looked like running into almost certain death, for aside from the six sentries there were hundreds of Moros within call.

"Bola mak no benga?" demanded Sergeant Hal, with an impudence and cool assurance that he was far from feeling.

One of the Moro sentries looked at the Army boys, grinning and shaking his head. Then laying two fingers across his mouth as a sign for silence, he pointed inside the mud-walled enclosure.

"Him hasta putti datto?" asked Hal, in a low voice.

"Datto" was the only word the Moro could make out, but he understood that, and again pointed inside.

"Banga tim no satti du," remarked Hal softly to his chum. Then Sergeant Hal bent low, making an elaborate bow before the gateway. Noll Terry "caught on" and followed suit. The Moro sentries grinned. Nor did they offer any objection when the Army boys strolled off into the tempest-ridden darkness.

"Now, what?" whispered Noll, as the Army boys halted under a tree.

"Noll, the biggest game in the world, now—to get back out of the trap into which we've stepped!"

CHAPTER XXIII
DOOMING THE DATTO

"Noll, you remember the first sentry inside the gully at this end?"

"Yes."

"Have you the nerve to stay near him while I try to get back to camp alone?"

"I have nerve enough to do anything that a soldier may be called upon to do."

"I was sure of it," Hal replied.

"But what's the game?"

"You are to keep close to that sentry until just before daylight," continued Hal. "Then, if nothing happens, slip out and make your way back to camp as best you can. But if Captain Freeman allows me to lead the expedition through that gully, you are to be on hand to silence that sentry at the first sound of our coming."

"I think I can do that," Sergeant Terry replied thoughtfully. "I'll either win out or give up my life without a murmur."

"Noll, if you prefer it, you can try to reach camp, and I'll stay by that first sentry inside the gully."

"No, Hal; I think you are far more apt to succeed in reaching camp than I. I'm satisfied with the second part in the game. Both parts are big enough."

"Very well! Good-bye, chum. Take care of yourself!"

They had yet a little distance to go before they came upon the Moro sentry beyond the inner mouth of the gully. As they approached him they strolled along in leisurely fashion.

The sentry, who appeared to be a good-natured, rather stupid fellow, surveyed the chums with a grin. He pointed to the sky, then made a motion of shivering. Clearly this native believed the pretended brown men to be foolish fellows for remaining out in such a downpour.

"Hastu maki not," observed Hal.

"No beni," replied Noll, and Hal stepped away in the darkness. He did not appear to be headed for the gully, but Noll distracted the attention of the sentry for a few moments, and out of the corner of his eye Terry caught a glimpse of Hal's body moving into the mouth of the gully.

A moment later Hal was out of sight and sound. Noll and the sentry stood side by side. Presently, as neither could understand the other's speech, Noll and the Moro fell to "conversing" by means of signs. Yet, in this line, they could go little beyond the weather. Noll presently made a hit with the real brown man by shaking his fist in the direction of the American camp, then drawing his hand across his throat with an eloquent gesture of throat-cutting.

Sergeant Hal Overton not only got out of the gully, but also satisfied himself that the slopes were not guarded.

"As the gully looks like a natural trap, and the datto has at least four hundred men between himself and the gully, I suppose old Hakkut is not worrying a great deal," reflected Overton.

Hal did not now trouble himself to move so stealthily, until he neared the American encampment. With noiseless step he approached and called out in the darkness:

"Officer of the day!"

"Halt! Who goes there?" called an alert soldier.

"Sergeant Overton, in scout disguise," Hal returned. "I wish to return to camp."

"Advance, Sergeant Overton, to be recognized."

Thus assured that he would not be shot down by mistake, Hal walked slowly but openly in the direction of the voice from the trench.

"If you can recognize me, Galbraith, you're a wonder," laughed Hal, as he came within the soldier's range of vision.

"*You*, Sergeant Overton. Great Scott, I don't recognize anything but the voice. I know that, however; pass on, Sergeant."

Hal went at once to Captain Freeman, whom, however, he had to awaken. Lieutenants Prescott and Holmes were quickly added to the lightning conference that followed.

The officers listened almost in amazement to the yarn that Sergeant Overton rapidly spun for them.

"We made no mistake in detailing you two sergeants to investigate the position of the enemy," remarked Captain Freeman warmly. "Now our course is clear. You understand my plan, gentlemen?"

The two young lieutenants quickly assented.

"We shall have to abandon our transport wagons, though I think we shall have no difficulty in recovering them later," went on the commanding officer. "Waken all the men, and have each man carry as much ammunition as he can pack. The Gatling gun goes with us, of course."

"And the wounded men, sir?" asked Lieutenant Prescott.

"Those still unable to walk will have to be carried on the same blanket stretchers. Caution these wounded men that, no matter what discomfort they may suffer on the trip, not one is to make a sound. Our lives are at stake. Now hustle, gentlemen! We must march from this position in less than twenty minutes."

"And the prisoners, sir?" asked Lieutenant Greg Holmes.

"Bind the prisoners and gag them, and do it effectively. We can't trust a prisoner on a dash like this. Leave them behind, but be sure that they can't effect their own escape. Gentlemen, I look to your effective aid in playing a most brilliant trick on the enemy."

Twelve minutes later the column started. They moved in three bodies. In advance were twelve picked men of B Company, under Sergeant Overton. Captain Freeman accompanied this little advance guard.

At a suitable interval behind marched fifty men under Lieutenant Prescott.

Last of all Lieutenant Holmes headed the remainder of the expedition. With this rear guard marched such of the wounded men as were able to walk. The others of the wounded were carried on blanket stretchers.

Silently, like a procession of ghosts, moved the American troops. The rain had moderated to a drizzle, but there was no star in sight to throw the least ray of light over the tropical scene.

Almost as straight as a bullet could have been fired Sergeant Hal led the advance guard to the mouth of the gully. There was no challenge, no shot fired by the enemy. A minute's halt; then the advance guard quickly followed Sergeant Overton into the gully, Captain Freeman stepping just behind the leader.

When they were two thirds of the way through, Sergeant Hal, who was still in his native costume, held up his hand as a signal to halt. The signal was passed back through the advance.

"I think you'd better wait here a few minutes, sir," whispered Hal to the commanding officer. "I'll hand my rifle to one of the men and then stroll forward to see if the coast is clear."

"A good plan, Sergeant; but take mighty good care of yourself!"

"Yes, sir. If you hear sounds of trouble up ahead then I suppose you'll push right on through."

"If there's any sound of trouble, whatever, Sergeant, you can depend upon our rushing through."

Saluting, Overton turned and slowly vanished into the darkness ahead. Just as he came out of the gully Hal heard a cautious, warning:

"Sh-sh!"

The muzzle of a rifle was thrust to his breast.

"Noll?" whispered Hal.

"Yes," whispered Terry.

"Where's the real sentry at this point?" breathed Hal.

"The poor fellow was chilled through. I got chummy with him, talking sign language, and then volunteered to stand duty for him. The Moro has gone off to take a sleep where it's drier."

"Bully, old Noll!"

"The troops are behind you, Hal?"

"Yes."

"Then march them ahead straight on for a hundred yards due west. You won't run into any of the enemy there. I've made it my business to know."

Hal flew back to the advance guard.

"Fine!" glowed Captain Freeman, when he had heard the report.

The advance was quickly in motion. Captain Freeman was soon up with Noll, who, after whispering, led the advance to the point he had mentioned to his chum. Hal, in the meantime, remained to receive and pilot Lieutenant Prescott's command.

"How on earth did you do this?" demanded Prescott in a whisper.

"Some of Sergeant Terry's work, sir," whispered Hal. "When you're ready, sir, just keep on straight ahead until you come upon the advance. I'll remain here, sir, if you permit, to warn the men behind you that they're marching inside the Moros' lines."

"Do so, Sergeant," directed Lieutenant Prescott, at the same time making the motion for his men to move ahead. On came the rest of the command in single file.

"Softly," warned Hal, as the men passed by him. "You're inside the enemy's lines."

Then, as the last man passed him, Hal whispered:

"Fall out, Gleason. Remain here to warn the rear guard when it arrives."

"All right, Sergeant. But this kind of work in the dark makes one creepy. I feel as though I were robbing a judge's chicken-roost."

Hal laughed softly and hurried after the vanishing troops. Within a few minutes more the rear guard had arrived.

By this time the rain had begun to come down again in torrents, but this favored the work of the American troops.

Led by the two young scouts, the entire command managed to advance, undetected, to a point from which Captain Freeman could dimly make out the mud walls of the datto's fort.

"Take the same twelve men of the advance guard, Sergeant Overton," whispered Captain Freeman, after he had given directions regarding the carrying of the wounded so that they would be as well protected as possible from slashing by Moro swords or creeses during the attack about to be made. "With your men, Sergeant, gain the gate of the fort. Remember, at no matter what cost, you must get your party inside and hold the gate. We'll be on the spot the moment we hear the first sound of your attack."

"Now, then, men," Hal instructed his own detachment, "we won't march forward, and we won't skulk, either. We'll simply stroll along. The instant that I hear any sound showing that we're discovered, I'll give the order to charge. When that order comes—remember that we simply must fight our way through the gate of the fort."

Then he gave the order for the forward movement. Hal placed himself at the head of his detachment, the post of greatest danger.

It was raining so heavily that even the guards at the datto's gate had relaxed their vigilance.

So Sergeant Hal Overton was within thirty feet of the gate when one of the six sentries, peering outside, caught sight of him, yelled and held his rifle at aim.

"Detachment charge!" yelled Sergeant Hal Overton.

With a low-uttered yet enthusiastic yell the twelve regulars piled in after their sergeant.

There was short, sharp firing at the gate. Then the Americans drove that guard in, killing four of them and holding the gate.

Now there was wild yelling inside the fort. Lights flashed from the principal building in the enclosure. Sergeant Hal waited only long enough to realize that Lieutenant Prescott's command had come up when he shouted to his own men:

"Follow me to the datto's house! He's the fellow we want."

Fifty natives howling wildly had thrown themselves around the house of the Datto Hakkut and had opened fire on the soldiers by the time that Hal and his few men reached the spot.

"Fight your way through 'em, men!" commanded Hal.

"Bring your men back, Sergeant!" shouted Captain Freeman in Hal's ear. "We've got the Gatling ready. I'll show you something better."

Swiftly the regulars dodged back. Sergeant Noll was at the breech of the Gatling.

R-r-r-r-rip! rattled out that rapid-fire machine, and the fire swept mercilessly into the ranks of those who defended the datto.

Lieutenant Holmes had gotten the wounded inside the walls. Now, with his efficient men he had turned to guard the gate, for outside, hundreds of frantically-yelling Moro fanatics had gathered for the attack on the invaders.

Into the closely packed ranks of the brown men who sought to defend the datto's house the Gatling poured its raking fire with fearful effect.

Whatever the issue of this madly fought battle, it began to look as though the Datto Hakkut were doomed.

CHAPTER XXIV
CONCLUSION

"Have your men fix their bayonets, Lieutenant Prescott!" commanded Captain Freeman. "Fall in, men! We'll take the datto on the rush!"

As the Moros, reinforced by two score more who had rushed to the aid of their leader, drew up for a last desperate stand before the house, the door opened.

A stream of light from inside illuminated the scene.

Out bounded a man past middle age and of imposing appearance. Not even his rich costume and flashing jewels were needed to proclaim that this man was the datto himself.

Behind Hakkut came another and younger man, the datto's sword-bearer.

Hakkut was carrying his own heavy, straight-edged sword. For a moment or two he stood blinking upon the scene of carnage and death below him as he halted on his porch. Then his gaze swept to the regulars behind the machine gun, standing alert with bayonets fixed, ready for that solitary word "charge!"

Instantly the datto turned and shouted something to the younger man with him.

In another moment the datto had placed the hilt of his sword against the flooring of the porch, the point of the weapon up. The younger man knelt swiftly, holding the sword in this position. Drawing back, the Datto Hakkut hurled himself forward with great force, falling upon the point. Then he tottered sideways, tumbling to the floor of the porch. The younger man without hesitation drove a needle-pointed creese three times into his ruler's breast. Withdrawing the knife, the sword-bearer then killed himself.

"Charge, Lieutenant Prescott!" called Captain Freeman.

"Charge!" repeated the lieutenant. The line of bayonets swept forward, but news of the death of the datto had already reached his would-be defenders. The regulars swept through, meeting little resistance, for hope had left the Moros with the passing of their savage prince.

In a twinkling the datto's house was in the hands of the regulars. Now a corporal's guard could have held it, for the Moros inside the fort who were still capable of fighting were throwing down their weapons in despair.

"Round the prisoners up, Lieutenant Prescott," commanded Captain Freeman. "I'll take some of your men and the Gatling to the gate to help Lieutenant Holmes."

In truth the Gatling was now sadly needed at the gate, for Lieutenant Holmes was having the fight of his life. Swarms of fanatic Moros were attempting to rush the small party of regulars.

The Gatling, placed in a position commanding the gate and sweeping all in front of it, soon checked the desperate attack at this point. The Moros could yet swarm the walls on all sides, however. The fight was far from won.

There was a chance still to close the huge wooden gate, and this Captain Freeman, with a few of his men, succeeded in doing just as the Gatling was withdrawn.

Suddenly it occurred to Captain Freeman that the night was passing and that the first dull light of day was creeping over the scene.

At the commanding officer's side Sergeant Hal Overton reported, saluting and saying:

"Sir, I have a suggestion to offer."

"State it, Sergeant."

"It seems like an almost dastardly thing to do, sir, but the death of the datto stopped the fighting inside. Wouldn't it be a good plan, sir, since the datto is assuredly dead, to have his body placed upon the top of the wall and hurled over to the Moros outside? When they behold that sight they may feel that their cause is gone."

"That is the best suggestion that could be made. You attend to it, Sergeant."

"Very good, sir."

Lieutenant Prescott paused for a moment in the shelter of the datto's porch. It had been warm work, and the young West Pointer was mopping his face with his handkerchief.

At this juncture Hal appeared with four men.

"Pardon me, sir," he said, saluting the lieutenant, "I am acting by Captain Freeman's orders."

With that the young sergeant pointed to the datto's body. The four men lifted it, carrying it from the porch. Prescott asked no question, but watched with interest what followed.

Across the yard Hal's squad bore the datto's body, to a point of the walls where the regulars were making their fiercest fight to repulse the Moros outside.

"Two of you climb up on the wall," Hal ordered. "The other two pass the body up."

This was done.

"Over with it," Sergeant Hal commanded, and the body was hurled to the ground outside.

An instant later there was a shout that was soon changed to a wail. In the growing daylight several of the Moro fighters had recognized the grisly message that had been hurled to them. Half a dozen fighting men dropped their weapons, picked up the datto's body and hurried off with it to a grove beyond.

Within two minutes the fighting had stopped. The Moros had fled to the grove, from which a loud, nerve-racking wailing now ascended.

Captain Freeman climbed to the top of the wall.

"We could wipe them out by the hundreds with the Gatling now," he remarked grimly. "However, I fancy it won't be necessary."

In half an hour the wailing of the Moros had ceased. They had gone farther away, and the regulars were content to remain behind the walls. While half of the effective troops were left on the walls, the other half prepared and ate their breakfast from the abundant food supplies found in the fort. After that the other half breakfasted.

That forenoon Lieutenant Holmes was sent out with a scouting force of thirty men. Two hours later he returned, stating that he had been unable to find any signs of the enemy.

In the afternoon Lieutenant Prescott and thirty men marched back to camp. There they found the transport wagons and horses uninjured, and returned with them to the fort after having set the half dozen native prisoners free.

"I fancy the cruel war is over, gentlemen," remarked Captain Freeman that evening to his two younger officers. "These Moros, like other semi-savages, fight with heart only when they have a great leader. In this way, the Datto Hakkut was a great man. For ten years he has been the scourge of northern Mindanao, but now we shall have a rest from him. He will never again disturb the peace of the island."

Early the following morning Lieutenant Prescott was sent out at the head of forty men, Hal and Noll accompanying him. Unless attacked by superior force this detachment was to remain out all day, scouting through the country for signs of the enemy.

In the morning two native villages were found close to the principal road through the mountains. As the natives appeared to have no weapons, and offered no trouble, they were not molested.

"You may be sure, though, Sergeant Overton," remarked Lieutenant Prescott, "that very nearly all of the men we have seen so far to-day served lately under the datto. However, if they have learned a lesson, and are now bent on peace, we won't molest them."

In the afternoon, as the detachment, moving at route step, reached the crest of a hill those in advance came upon a party of Moros camped in a grove by the road. These men, perhaps fifty in number, were preparing a meal. They displayed no weapons.

"These men were undoubtedly recent fighters, too," remarked Lieutenant Prescott. "However, we'll look them over to make sure that they have no weapons now."

Hardly had the two sergeants started on their tour of inspection when one man leaped suddenly from his seat on the ground and made off on a run.

"There's the man we want!" yelled Hal. "Vicente Tomba, I call upon you to halt and surrender!"

But Tomba, for it was he, continued to run fleetly.

"Bring that man down, if he won't stop!" commanded Lieutenant Prescott sternly.

"Halt, Tomba, or we fire!" shouted Hal. "Ready, men! Aim! fire!"

Seven rifles spoke, almost in unison. Vicente Tomba pitched forward, then fell. When examined he was found to have received four bullet wounds. As he was dead, the soldiers buried him then and there.

"Men who are found in Tomba's company are subjects for suspicion," remarked Lieutenant Prescott dryly. "Though we've found no weapons with this crowd we'll round 'em up and take 'em in."

This was done. Captain Freeman decided to read these natives a lesson and then let them go.

"Why not make the rascals most humbly salute the Flag, sir?" suggested Sergeant Overton respectfully. "I still have the Flag that the Moros insulted."

"A good idea," nodded the commanding officer. "Get the Flag, Sergeant."

Over the late datto's fort the Stars and Stripes soon fluttered. The troops were paraded to do the emblem honor. Then the Moro prisoners were forced to pay it humble reverence, after which they were allowed, on their hands and knees, to crawl out of the fort and find their liberty outside.

"I'm sorry the datto didn't live a little longer," murmured Sergeant Hal to his chum. "I'd have enjoyed seeing him salute the Flag fifty times and then crawl away on his knees."

The following morning Captain Freeman marched his column back over the many miles that lay between them and Bantoc. On a later morning of the march the dusty column passed Draney's plantation. That adventurer boldly hailed the officers as the troops marched by.

"I hear you've killed the datto," was the planter's greeting.

"Yes," responded Captain Freeman dryly. "There are a few others, though, who deserve the same fate."

"We'll mix it up with that scoundrel yet," muttered Hal to his chum.

Back in Bantoc all was quiet again. Cerverra had been released with a reprimand that he was not likely to forget. Now that the datto was gone, the spirit was lacking for insurrection, and that part of Mindanao settled down to quiet.

For how long? Undoubtedly the reader will discover in the next volume of this series—a volume that will be filled with the lively doings of our Army in the Philippines. This great tale will be published under the title, "Uncle Sam's Boys on Their Mettle; Or, A Chance to Win Officers' Commissions." In this forthcoming narrative the reader will meet several old friends and will renew their acquaintance in the most startling situations.

The End

CPSIA information can be obtained at www.ICGtesting.com
Printed in the USA
LVOW10s1604020214

371970LV00031B/1408/P

9 781492 123415